Sapphire Mage

OTHER BOOKS BY DOROTHY DREYER

Phoenix Descending

Paragon Rising

Cauldron of Ash

THE EMPIRE OF THE LOTUS SERIES

Crimson Mage

Copper Mage

Golden Mage

Emerald Mage

COMING SOON

Amethyst Mage

Diamond Mage

SAPPHIRE

Mage

EMPIRE OF THE LOTUS
BOOK FIVE

DOROTHY DREYER

Sapphire Mage
Empire of the Lotus Book Five

Copyright © 2020 Dorothy Dreyer
Edited by Amy McNulty
Cover design by Sora Sanders

Published November 2020 by Snowy Wings Publishing
PO Box 1035, Turner, OR 97392

For hope in this ever-changing world

In the battle to save the world, things have taken a fatal turn.

The elite mages have succeeded in getting ahead of Kashmeru's shadow army, but now the power has shifted, and the good guys have taken a hit. It's up to Jae and the rest of the crew to outwit the Pishacha and take back what they've lost.

Loyalties are tested and resilience pushed to the limits, as the war continues between the divine and evil.

The open sky sits upon our senses
like a sapphire crown – the Air is
our robe of state – the Earth is our
throne, and the Sea a mighty
minstrel playing before it.
– John Keats

The legend goes …

The ancient deity Kashmeru knew only one true love—the Lotus empress Lakshmi, who in his eyes possessed all beauty and grace the universe could hold. Their hearts called to one another, a hold so strong that neither one could deny the bond. But Lakshmi knew that Kashmeru's spirit was not pure, for an evil dwelled within his soul, a wickedness so corrupt that it could destroy the universe.

And when she denied him her love, destroying the universe was the very thing he vowed to do.

Throughout the centuries, their reincarnations were drawn to one another, but the outcome was always the same: Lakshmi would never give Kashmeru her heart.

To put an end to his constant chase, the Empire of the Lotus defeated Kashmeru and sealed him in a tomb using mage powers, where he would remain trapped …

… until the Council of the Seven could secure the blood of the Lotus empress to set him free.

THE SEVEN HOUSES OF MAGES

Crimson: earth, stability, survival, security.

Copper: water, ice, pleasure, guilt.

Golden: fire, willpower, shame.

Emerald: air, wind, heart, love, grief.

Sapphire: throat, sound, truth, lies.

Amethyst: vision, sight, illusions, secrets.

Diamond: spirituality, emotion, virtue, integrity.

One

Park Jae-hyun let out a sigh of relief when the cars finally reached the temple. Jae had spent the entire drive checking the side mirror while Mayhara had driven. He couldn't believe their luck; they hadn't been followed. Both cars had safely raced away from the celebrations at the governor's mansion before anyone could discover that the Pishacha and dark mages had been trapped in one of the rooms. Of course, the spell that had trapped them there had to have been broken by now. It had only lasted as long as Karina's enchanted candle burned. Which was why Jae's eyes had been trained on the road behind both getaway cars.

Mayhara shut off the engine once they were parked and glanced at Jae. Her long, dark hair fell softly over her cheeks. Things were still tense between them, and Jae felt a vise tightening around his heart. She had been hurt because he hadn't disclosed the truth about his past relationship with Loni. She'd basically ended whatever had been growing between them before it could really even begin. He desperately wanted to find a time to sit down with her and explain himself. To tell her how he truly felt about her. But she continually brushed him off, stating that she needed to concentrate on their mission. Their relationship was purely professional now. Just two members of the band of mages who vowed to protect the legacy of the Empire of the Lotus and prevent the dark god Kashmeru from destroying the world. No big deal.

Shiro, who had been driving the other car, nodded to Jae once, pushing back the strands of his black and copper hair as he sighed. The expression on his face was one of concern. Jae figured Shiro must have felt the same as he did about their escape from the party: uncertain and skeptical about their victory. They'd been successful in acquiring the daggers, but that didn't mean they'd won the battle. They still had to find and rescue Naree—Jae's sister, who was the reincarnation of the Lotus empress—and break the spell she was under. The dark god Kashmeru was controlling her every move, using the lure of their centuries-long, complicated, love-hate relationship to manipulate her to do his bidding. He needed her to break the spell that kept him locked in a cursed tomb. But he couldn't be released without the arcane daggers.

And the mages now had all seven.

Mayhara averted her gaze when Jae caught her looking at him. The hair on the nape of his neck stiffened as she turned and headed for the temple entrance without a word. Jae, Shiro, Yuki, and Loni followed Mayhara toward the door. The skirts of the ball gowns Yuki and Loni wore swished as they walked.

But then, Yuki suddenly stopped.

Jae and Shiro turned to her when they noticed her standing frozen, her face pale against her auburn hair. The other mages stopped to study her as well. She wrapped her arms around her middle and shivered.

"What is it?" Jae asked. "What's wrong?"

"Fear." Yuki bit her lip. "I feel fear, coming from inside the temple. And… something else. I think it's… death."

Jae and the others widened their eyes, their bodies tensing.

"Amalia," Mayhara said with panic in her voice. She turned on her heel and bolted into the temple.

Jae was close behind, the others in tow. He silently prayed to the gods that Amalia—the swamp witch who'd saved Shiro's life—was all right. Her blood had been poisoned by a dark mage, and despite Shiro's attempts at using his powers to syphon out the poison, Amalia was getting worse.

If she was dead…

The mages burst into the temple and began to search for the others who had stayed behind. But their search stopped short when Loni screamed in the living room. The rest of the mages hurried to find her.

Loni, looking pale as she stood, trembled, with her

dark waves falling from her hair clip, her hands covering her mouth, and tears flowing down her cheeks.

Jae gasped at what was on the floor in front of her.

"Kamal!" Mayhara rushed to the body sprawled out on the cold marble floor surrounded by a pool of blood.

Jae bent down beside the long form of Kamal's body and immediately used his sapphire powers to listen for breathing or a heartbeat. Neither one could be found.

"He's dead," Yuki whispered. "His spirit has left him."

As the diamond mage, Yuki would have been able to sense his spirit. If Jae had doubted himself about not hearing a pulse, he would have to believe Yuki's words. Their sapphire elite was dead.

"What... What happened here?" Shiro looked around.

The place was in a shambles, furniture knocked over, drawers ripped from cabinets, and the sofa torn to shreds. Even paintings had been stripped from the walls.

"They were here," Jae said. "They found the temple, and they were looking for the daggers."

"And they killed Kamal in the process." Loni's voice broke on their fellow mage's name.

"Where are the others?" Mayhara stood with her hands clutched to her chest and ran to the hall.

They all followed her to Amalia's room, but when they arrived at where her door should have been, they discovered it gone. The mages looked around at each other in confusion.

"What happened to her door?" Loni asked. "This doesn't make sense."

"Sight," Mayhara said, feeling the wall where the door used to be. "Penny must have cloaked the door with her amethyst powers."

Jae watched as Mayhara's hand clamped around a space of air.

"I found the knob." Mayhara jostled at it and then shook her head. "It's locked."

Yuki placed her hands on the invisible door, her palms glowing white. "They are in there. They're afraid. That's the fear I felt."

Jae lifted his palms, the blue glow reflecting off the wall where the door was hidden. He didn't know if Penny's cloaking spell had blocked the sound out, but he had to let the others inside Amalia's room know they were there.

"Hello, can you hear me? It's Jae." He pushed his sound powers through the wall. "Darshana? Penny? Salina? Are you in there?"

Still using his powers, he heard Karina—Amalia's granddaughter—swallow hard. The sound of a chair screeching against the floor followed.

"Jae! Yes!" Karina answered. "We're here."

"Can you unlock the door?" Jae asked. "Or is it spelled shut?"

In a few seconds, the lock clicked, and a wide-eyed Karina opened the door, which magically materialized before their eyes. Karina gasped in surprise, pushing her dark, unkempt hair away from her face.

The mages rushed inside. Mayhara first embraced a trembling Darshana and then Salina, Shiro crouched down next to the bed to feel the sleeping Amalia's forehead, and Loni asked Mr. Kitaro—the Sacred Key, keeper of one of the magic daggers—what had happened.

"We're not sure what happened," Mr. Kitaro said. "Penny told us to keep quiet and lock the door. We heard a lot of ruckus, but we followed her instructions."

Jae, Shiro, and Mayhara exchanged glances.

"They found the temple," Loni explained. "The Pishacha. Or the dark mages. Or both. And they… they killed Kamal."

Karina slapped a hand over her mouth and backed up against the wall. Darshana closed her eyes and bowed her head, her mouth drawn into a frown. Mr. Kitaro ran a hand down his face. Salina's jaw hung open in shock.

"They must have been searching for the daggers," Jae added.

"Wait." Mayhara's head whipped around. "Where's Penny?"

Two

There was a buzzing in Penny's head. Like wires transferring electricity, each pulse a dull ache in her temples. Her eyes slowly drifted open, and she found a pair of dark eyes staring back at her. The face was unfamiliar, the young man's mouth kept in a straight line. Her eyes drifted momentarily to the scar running from one eyebrow to his cheekbone.

"She's awake," he said, looking over his shoulder as he

stood upright. "Ru, get Bhutano."

The girl he spoke to looked up from filing her jet-black nails and wrinkled her lip in response. She tucked away the nail file and headed for the metallic door. With a wave of her hand, which emitted tendrils of black smoke, the door opened for her, closing as soon as she stepped outside the room.

Penny took in a deep breath, remembering what had happened. The dark mages and Naree had infiltrated the temple... and killed Kamal. She swallowed hard, remembering the blood. Her head spun, and the spot on her head where she'd been struck throbbed.

Something sharp and metallic pierced the skin at her wrists when she tried to move. She figured they were electro-cuffs that bound her wrists together behind her back, securing her to the chair she'd woken up in. She bit back the panic that rose in her throat. It wouldn't improve her situation to lose her calm. Plus, she needed to minimize her movements. She didn't want to feel the shock of the cuffs if she were to try to get free.

She glanced around the room, taking in the six remaining figures spread out in the cold, dimly lit, windowless space. Was she in a basement? She couldn't tell.

Penny recognized the only female of the seven—the one who had left the room—as the daughter of Director Shei, head of the census division of the government. Mayhara had been the one to put the pieces of that puzzle together. From what Penny could gather, Ru had telekinetic abilities, able to move things with her dark mage powers. With her straight, black hair hanging in her face and her ever-present frown, Ru was the gloomiest looking one out of the seven.

Penny's focus shifted over to two of the dark mages who stood together on one side of the room. They whispered something to each other that Penny couldn't hear. She recognized these two from the news. Avi was the governor's son. With his wild hair, boyish face, and thick lips, Avi was easily the best-looking of the group, and Penny could understand why Yuki had fallen for him. Beside Avi was Harish, the son of the richest family in New Jaipur. The wildness in his eyes overshadowed his prominent nose and thick brows.

The one with the scar on his cheek moved into her line

of vision. He gave her a cynical sneer as he leaned closer to her. "Where are your friends to help you out now, mage?"

"Daiki," Avi called. "Get out of her face. Bhutano said to back off until he talks to her."

Daiki twisted his mouth sideways and ran a hand roughly over his mop of messy hair. "Yeah, whatever."

She wasn't familiar with Daiki, and a glance at the others told her how uneducated she was on the dark mages. She made a note to try to read them with her powers when they lowered their guard.

The door to the room opened again, and Ru stomped in. She plopped down on a chair and lifted her feet, her heavy boots coming down hard to rest on a small table. Entering the room behind her were the chief of police—whom the mages recently learned was being possessed by Kashmeru's evil spirit messenger, Bhutano—followed by Naree—the reincarnation of the Lotus Empress Lakshmi.

The chief of police was impressive, with his pristine uniform, impeccable coifed hair, and perfect posture, but it was Naree whom Penny was mesmerized by. Penny could tell from Naree's eyes and cheekbones that she was Jae's sister. The family resemblance was unmistakable. But

Naree also had an allure about her, like she was made up of pure magic. Her wavy, brunette hair fell loosely over her temples, and there was a magical draw to her chestnut brown eyes. Penny had seen her before, of course, but never this closely.

Harish stepped forward and placed a chair opposite Penny, which Naree sat in, her eyes locked with Penny's. Harish then strode back to join the other dark mages as they witnessed whatever it was Bhutano had planned to do.

"Hello, Penny," Bhutano said, pacing beside her with his hands clasped behind his back. "You might be wondering why we didn't simply kill you along with your fellow mage back at the temple."

Penny shifted her gaze from Bhutano back to Naree.

"It might have crossed my mind," Penny answered.

"Yes," he continued, "well, we went to the temple with the intention of collecting what belongs to us. But you surprised us by being clever enough to hide them where even the most powerful being could not see."

They didn't find the daggers?

Penny dropped her gaze. She knew she had to be very

careful around Naree. Naree had all the powers every class of mage had. That included amethyst mage powers—vision, insight, illusions, and secrets. If she used her powers, she could see what Penny was thinking. She could find out their secrets. She had to clear her mind as much as possible so Naree wouldn't see.

"I could feel the magic of the daggers," Naree said. "But their exact location was fuzzy in my mind. It was as if a witch had cast a cloaking spell on them."

Again, Penny pushed all thoughts from her head. She didn't want the enemy to find out about Karina. They'd already poisoned Karina's grandmother. She had to keep Karina safe from their destructive ways.

"We searched the temple, so perhaps they were in another location." Naree held out her hands. Her palms glowed with bright blue light.

Truth, Penny realized.

"Where are the daggers, Penny?" Naree asked.

Penny felt the pull of Naree's power. Though she tried not to speak at all, there was no fighting the force of the sapphire powers Naree used on her.

"I don't know." Penny's eyes widened at her own

words. She didn't know. Penny realized what she'd said was actually the truth. The daggers had been moved. They weren't where she remembered them to be.

Logically, it made sense. There was no doubt that when the other elites discovered Kamal's body, they would have realized the temple was no longer safe and decided to move to a different location, bringing the daggers with them. And since she had no idea where the mages would have gone, she was clueless as to where the daggers were.

She paused, the thought of Kamal filling her thoughts. Her heart tightened up, like it was being crushed beneath a heavy weight. Kamal was dead. They'd killed him.

And now they were holding her prisoner, sparing her life only if she could give them some answers.

"What do you mean, you don't know?" Bhutano asked, his jaw tight with anger.

"At this point, I don't know where the daggers are." Penny lifted her chin. "They've been moved. I don't know the new location."

"But you can use your insight to find out," Naree said, her voice calm.

Penny tilted her head. "You know as well as I do that

the daggers are cloaked in magic."

Naree pursed her lips. "But you were able to track them down before."

Penny didn't offer an answer. The blue glow returned to Naree's palms.

"Meditation." Penny let out a sigh, finding it too hard to fight the sapphire mage power of truth. "It takes time."

As Naree studied Penny's face, something occurred to Penny. Naree hadn't been to the academy. She hadn't learned the ins and outs of mage powers like the mages who had attended the academy had. Although Naree held all the power of each class of mage, she wasn't trained in using them. She didn't know the rules.

"It's possible for me to track them down," Penny said. "But I'm not exactly in the ideal mindset or physical comfort to do that." She gestured at her arms, still bound behind her back.

Naree glanced at Bhutano. He stopped pacing and gave Naree a single nod.

"Perhaps we can arrange something," Naree said. "But understand this. I will be able to see your visions. Any information you try to conceal in that pretty little head of yours will be found out. So there's no use trying to hide it."

Penny took a deep breath, holding Naree's gaze. There was more at stake than just the daggers she needed to keep hidden from the Pishacha. She forced herself not to think about the grimoire. If the Lotus used her amethyst powers to see Penny's thoughts, she might find out about their plans to get the grimoire, and she needed to stop the enemy from gaining any more advantages.

Three

The somber mood in the air was almost tangible. Jae followed Mr. Kitaro along with the rest of the group. They carried with them what they could from the temple, the weight of their belongings nothing compared to the weight of losing Kamal.

With the Pishacha having discovered the location of the temple, the group would have been sitting ducks if they'd remained. And just because the dark mages hadn't been able to find the daggers on their first ambush of the place, that didn't mean they wouldn't return and do everything in their power to find them on a subsequent visit.

They were at a loss as to where to go, and so Mr. Kitaro had suggested a safehouse he had tucked away in a remote area just outside the city. Jae glanced back at Shiro, who was helping Karina get Amalia down the concealed path that led to the safehouse. The cars and Jae's bike were hidden behind a cluster of trees and bushes not far from the house, but the short walk, which progressed through rocky and uneven terrain, felt like miles to Jae.

None of them had had any sleep since before the festival. And the adrenalin rush after finding Kamal dead and Penny missing was quickly fading.

Up ahead, walking beside Darshana, Mayhara cast a quick glance over her shoulder at him. Their eyes only met for a second, but in that small moment, Jae felt his heart being crushed. She'd barely spoken to him since their fight. And of course, with everything that had happened since she'd told him she couldn't be with him, there were more urgent things to deal with. But still, he longed to have a heart-to-heart with her and let her know how he felt about her.

Salina reached the door to the cabin right after Mr. Kitaro. She looked back at the crew and let out a sigh. Though her posture showed she was as exhausted as the rest of the group, there was a fire in her eyes that told Jae she was prepared to fight for their cause. To go to any lengths to get Penny back. She'd lost enough. They all had.

"It's modest," Mr. Kitaro said as they all caught up and gathered on the front porch. "But it's off the grid, and, as you could probably tell from the trek here, virtually impossible to find."

Jae was going to mention how well the temple had been hidden as well before it had been found, but he bit back his words. He needed to think more positive if he was going to get through this.

As if she could sense his struggle, Darshana cast him a glance.

Mr. Kitaro flipped open a control panel beside the door and punched a code into the lock pad. The light on the lock pad changed from red to green, and Mr. Kitaro opened the door.

"I just need to turn on the main generator to get the power up," Mr. Kitaro said.

There were a few clicks of metal Jae couldn't see. In the next second the lights inside automatically came on as Mr. Kitaro stepped into the house.

"As I mentioned, it's not as grand as the temple. Rooms will have to be shared."

"I'm sure we'll manage," Mayhara said, offering him a thankful smile.

Mr. Kitaro placed a hand on Karina's shoulder. "I think the first room down the hall on the right would suit Amalia and you. We should get her settled."

"Thank you," Karina said.

Amalia, whose eyes were droopy, gave him a slight nod. Her jaw was tense and her grip on her granddaughter was tight.

"I'll help them settle in," Shiro told him.

Loni and Yuki squeezed past Jae, and when Yuki caught Jae's eyes, he wondered if she was using her diamond mage powers to read his emotions. Salina had paired up with Mayhara and disappeared down the hall.

Jae set down the motorcycle helmets and glanced around the quaint space, stretching out his back muscles. "This place is actually nice."

"It's safe." Mr. Kitaro pointed to the windows in the living room. "Bulletproof glass." He moved over to a monitor near the kitchen and swiped the screen. The monitor came to life, showing four different views of their surroundings. "Hidden cameras set up around the perimeter with silent alarms that will alert us if anyone trespasses."

"Great setup."

"I take the position of Sacred Key seriously. Though I haven't had the opportunity to use this place as a sanctuary until now."

"Yeah, speaking of which…" Jae ran a hand over the stubble on his chin. "Do you think this place is safe enough to hide the daggers?"

Mr. Kitaro placed his hands on his sides. "I spoke with Darshana about it. Neither of us are one hundred percent certain it's a good idea. If the Pishacha do manage to track us down, the chances of them finding the daggers could sway in their favor. Darshana decided to meditate on it as soon as she gets settled. We'll have a meeting once everyone is rested and decide what to do. Together."

Jae nodded. "Sounds good. I guess I'll go see if any beds are left and settle in."

With a sigh, he made his way down the hall where the rooms were located. Karina, Amalia, and Darshana were in the first room. The door was open, and Jae spotted Karina propping the pillows in the bed Amalia lay in. Darshana pulled the comforter over Amalia's legs, her brows low in worry.

Farther down the hall, Yuki and Loni were unpacking in the room they'd claimed. Jae noticed there was a third bed in their room and suspected they were being optimistic about finding Penny. He hoped they were right.

Yuki turned to face Jae, though he hadn't made a sound. Loni didn't seem to notice when Yuki headed toward the door to approach Jae. He took a step back as she continued into the hall and closed the door behind her.

"She's hanging on by a thread," Yuki whispered. She held up her hand and opened it to reveal the white glow in her palm. "I'm doing what I can to keep her grounded, but it's exhausting. I think it's best if you give her some space. Her emotions really go out of whack when you're around, and I just don't have it in me to stop that rollercoaster."

Jae nodded solemnly. "Understood. Thank you for watching out for her."

She gave a half-shrug. "Just doing my part." She studied his face. "You're a cluster of turmoil and anxiety yourself. Let me know if you need some time with me, just to calm your nerves."

"Thanks." He offered her a small smile. "I'll be okay."

She nodded before returning to her room, and Jae continued down the hall. He almost collided with Mayhara as she exited the room she was sharing with Salina. She took a step back, breathing in deeply and stuffing her hands in her pockets as she averted her eyes. He wanted so much to embrace her and tell her how much he missed her company, but he refrained.

"Hey," he said.

"Hey." Her voice was soft. She glanced up at him, her thick lashes hiding the full view of her eyes.

"You all right?"

She shrugged as she nodded. "As best as I can be, under the circumstances. Torn up over Kamal and hoping Penny is okay."

"Yeah. Me too." He glanced down the hall. "Mr. Kitaro said we're going to meet later to talk about where to keep the daggers."

"That's a good idea. It's crucial we keep them out of reach of the Pishacha. And the fact that we have them all means those targets on our backs just got a lot bigger."

"Normally, I'd take a shot at brainstorming and making a list of possibilities, but I'm just too—"

"Exhausted." Mayhara let out a sigh. "Yeah, me too."

For a moment, they stood in silence, their locked eyes speaking volumes. The second Jae worked up the courage to breach the topic of their feelings, Mayhara took a step back.

"I'm going to…" She pointed over her shoulder. "I'd like to get a shower in before we all meet with Darshana."

"Oh." He rubbed the back of his neck. "Okay."

She turned and disappeared into her room, closing the door behind her. Jae had to clear his throat in order to swallow back his disappointment.

Everything seemed to be pressing in on him. He hoped the buzzing in his head was just a side effect from exhaustion mixed with his emotions being pushed to extremes. The alternative would be that his powers were on the fritz.

At the end of the hall, Jae found a room to the right and one to the left.

"That one's Mr. Kitaro's," Shiro said, poking his head through the doorway on the right. "You can room with me if you want."

"Perfect. Just point me in the direction of my bed. If I could just close my eyes for twenty minutes, I might be able to keep them from popping out of my head."

"Yeah, good idea." Shiro's mouth formed a slight smirk. "Not even you could pull off that look."

Four

Darshana sat at the dining room table, her hands splayed, palms down, on the tabletop. Her eyes were open, but Jae could tell her focus was elsewhere. Experience told him she was trying to hold on to the visions she must have seen when she'd meditated.

Yuki and Loni were already seated near Darshana. The warning look Yuki flashed Jae caused him to pick a seat far from Loni. Mayhara and Karina were next to join them. To his surprise, Mayhara sat across from Jae. Karina hovered near the kitchen island behind the dining room table. Mr. Kitaro strode in, looking dignified as always, and took the seat next to Darshana.

Shiro gave everyone a nod as he entered the room and went immediately to Karina's side. "How's Amalia?"

Karina shook her head and crossed her arms over her chest. "She seems worse. She's resting now, but even in her sleep, she looks like she's suffering."

Shiro placed a hand on her arm. "I'll come see her after this and try to help her a little."

She mouthed a *thank you* that didn't quite hit the air.

As soon as he sat down, Salina rushed into the room. Her eyes were wide and frantic. "Your pictures just hit the news sites."

Jae held his hands up, as if to slow her down. "Wait. What's going on? Whose pictures?"

She slid into a chair. "Yours. And Yuki's and Loni's. They've pegged you for an attempted terrorist attack on the governor's mansion."

Almost all of them whipped out their Linqs to check the web. Jae's jaw dropped when an image of his face appeared with the label "Fugitive" in one of the news reports. Next to him were images of Loni and Yuki.

"How did they know it was us?" he asked. "We had masks on at the ball."

"Because the Imperial Police are working with the Pishacha," Mayhara said. "And Naree knows it was you."

"It probably didn't take much to figure out who the others were," Mr. Kitaro added. "Especially if they obtained information from the academy. Or if they used Naree's amethyst powers."

"Great," Loni mumbled.

"It doesn't matter," Yuki said. "We already knew we'd have to go into hiding. This doesn't change anything."

"Except that we can't show our faces in public anymore." Loni tucked her Linq away. "It's going to make things a lot harder."

Darshana waited for them to settle down, keeping her chin high and her expression blank. They all seemed to notice she wanted to speak, so they stilled their voices and sat attentively. It was like being back at the academy again.

Darshana placed her hands together, her eyes meeting each elite mage, one by one. "I'll start with the good news.

Penny is alive."

"You found her?" Loni asked, leaning forward in her chair.

"Not exactly." Darshana ran a finger from her temple down to her jaw, her gaze elsewhere. "I felt her presence. She's afraid, which tells me the Pishacha have her. But she's still alive, which tells me they need her for something."

"The daggers," Mayhara said. "They want her to tell them where they are."

"But we've taken them with us," Salina said. "She doesn't know where they are."

"She's an amethyst mage," Jae put in. "She can find them with her mind. She's done it before."

"Which means she's got every right to be afraid," Mayhara added. "The dark mages will likely do whatever it takes to get that information from her."

"She won't tell," Loni insisted. "Even if it costs her her life."

"On the other hand…" Shiro glanced at Karina for a split second. "It's reasonable to assume they won't kill her. As long as she withholds any information from them."

"Unless their methods of torture break her down." Karina's gaze was trained on the floor. "Cause her pain until she can't withhold from them anymore."

Jae knew Karina was thinking about what the dark mages had done to her grandmother. They'd poisoned her, threatening to leave her for dead if they didn't give them the information they'd wanted. Of course, Amalia had refused, which was why she was lying in her bed suffering. Even Shiro's blood syphoning wasn't working to get rid of the poison. It just kept reproducing and growing inside her.

If the dark mages poisoned Penny to get her to talk, she might not be able to keep the location of the daggers a secret.

"Which is why," Darshana said, "I've come up with an idea of what to do with the daggers."

Everyone waited with anticipation for Darshana to continue. Jae would have held his breath if his heart hadn't been hammering so hard.

"The Sacred Keys separated the daggers for a reason." Darshana gave Mr. Kitaro a nod. "If the daggers are not all in one place, it will make it harder for the enemy to find. I propose that we follow the Keys' logic and do as they did."

"Meaning?" asked Shiro.

"Meaning the six of you should each take a dagger and find an undisclosed location for it without telling the others where it's hidden—just as the Sacred Keys did."

"This makes sense, especially now," Mr. Kitaro added, "because of the possibility of the Pishacha getting Penny to use her powers to track down the daggers."

Darshana gave a nod. "She won't be able to see them all at once or try to get into any one person's head to find them."

"That's true," Yuki said, leaning forward in her chair. "It took her a while to track down each dagger before we found them. And even then, we were too late for some of them."

Darshana let out a slow breath. "Does everyone agree?"

Everyone nodded, looking around at each other. Jae's mind scrambled to think of a place to hide the dagger he'd be given. It would have to be somewhere clever, somewhere the Pishacha wouldn't think to look.

"I'd like them hidden as soon as possible," Darshana said. "You don't have to stick to Mr. Kitaro's property, but please do take care when traveling elsewhere to keep out of sight, and make sure you are not followed." Darshana let out a breath. "Mr. Kitaro will find a place for the seventh dagger in Penny's absence."

Everyone seemed deep in thought for a moment, no doubt trying to figure out where to hide the daggers.

After a moment, Darshana spoke up again. "We have another problem: the grimoire. What we need to do now is find the grimoire before the Pishacha find out about it from Penny."

Jae raised his hand. "I'll go. I've been to Pune before, and I think getting there on my bike will be easier than in a car."

"I'll go with him," Mayhara said.

Jae studied her face, but she kept her eyes on Darshana. He caught Loni's eyes shifting between them, but he quickly averted his gaze.

Jae cleared his throat. "Okay, good. We can leave in the morning. Get a fresh start. It's a long drive."

Darshana placed her hands together. "Very well. I'm

going to try reaching out to Penny again."

"If you can locate her," Salina said, "we'll be ready to go in for a rescue."

"Yeah." Loni raked her hands through her dark hair. "Count me in. I'll do anything to get her back."

Jae glanced around at everyone. There was one more pressing issue on his mind. "I wanted to bring up what I heard the chief of police and Director Shei discussing at the ball."

"You mean about the prison camps?" Yuki asked.

"Yeah." Jae rubbed at his chin. "Anyone have any ideas of what we can do about it?"

Shiro lifted his hand. "Maybe I can reach out, try to find Qiang. He could have some intel on what's happening at the prison camps—or could at least find out. If we know the government's strategy, we might be able to figure out how to stop them."

"Good idea." Darshana breathed in deeply and let out a slow breath. "There's one more thing. Something that came to me while I was searching for a sign of Penny."

Mayhara furrowed her brow. "What was it?"

"It's about the comet." Darshana's expression was

troubled. "The vision of it appeared to me, and with it, a strange, pulsing, static energy. It was like waves of power disrupting everything it touched. I focused on it further and understood that its energy conflicted with the energy of mages. Like polar opposites ricocheting off each other."

Yuki tilted her head. "What does that mean?"

"I believe," Darshana said, "as the comet gets closer, it will interfere with your powers."

"You think it will leave us powerless?" Jae asked.

Darshana shook her head. "I don't know. I don't think it's a permanent effect, but rather something that will occur as the comet is in close proximity."

Mayhara shifted in her chair. "Is that why the prophecy mentions Kashmeru being reborn upon the comet's arrival? Because our powers will be weak?"

Shiro scratched at an eyebrow. "Giving Kashmeru and the Pishacha power over us."

Darshana and Mr. Kitaro exchanged looks.

"Yes," Mr. Kitaro answered. "I believe it is so."

"Well, that sucks." Loni threw her hands in the air. "How are we supposed to fight them if we're stripped of our powers?

"I hope it doesn't come to that," Darshana said, "But if it does, then by any means necessary that will keep things balanced in our favor. The time has come to tie up any loose ends. Get the grimoire. Hide the daggers. And figure out a way to get the Lotus out of Kashmeru's grip."

Five

The morning sun filtered through the gauzy curtains as a slight breeze brought fresh air to play with Naree's hair. She sat at her vanity, holding a hairbrush and studying her face. Her skin was flawless, her hair thick and lustrous. She wore a silk robe and her bedroom floor was heated. She'd slept comfortably and had a delicious-smelling breakfast waiting for her downstairs.

This was the life Kashmeru was offering her. He promised to always take care of her, and he was keeping that promise.

My love.

"Kashmeru."

I can feel the time nearing when we can be together.

"Yes. I've made some progress."

You have all the daggers?

She bit her lip and set down the hairbrush. "Almost"

There was a pause, and Naree's nerves tightened. For all the love she felt, why did Kashmeru frighten her? She stood from the vanity and began to pace, worrying her hands.

You need to hurry, my love. The comet is approaching.

"I'm doing my best."

Please do. It won't be long before we'll be together and I can hold you in my arms again.

"I know. I long for that as well. I promise, I'm doing my best."

Six

The hot shower did wonders for Jae's exhaustion, but it hadn't made a dent in the anxiety that clung to every inch of him. He pulled on a clean T-shirt and raked his fingers through his thick, dark hair. As he took his hand away, he focused on his fingers. Darshana's words about the comet's influence on their powers replayed in his mind. He didn't feel any different, magic-wise. He wondered how close the comet had to be in order to feel the effect.

Stepping out into the main room, he found Darshana standing by the window, sipping tea. Nearby, in the open kitchen, Loni was pouring herself a cup. She only spared him a glance.

"Heading out?" Darshana asked when she turned to face him.

"It's a long drive." He grabbed his leather jacket, which hung over a dining room chair. "As it is, we won't get there until tomorrow. The sooner we leave, the better. I'm just waiting for Mayhara."

Loni turned toward him and leaned back against the counter, staring into her tea.

"Jae." Darshana took a breath and let it out calmly. "We haven't really spoken about your newly inherited station."

Jae rubbed his chin as he nodded. "Elite sapphire mage. Yeah. I've, uh, been trying to wrap my head around it."

"Yes, I know." Darshana stepped closer to him. "I can feel your struggle."

Jae and Loni exchanged a glance. Loni raised a brow

and sipped her tea.

"You feel it?" Jae slipped the jacket on and adjusted the collar. "Sounds a little diamond-mage-ish."

"She's an empath," Loni put in. "Why do you think she's making me drink this disgusting tea?"

Jae furrowed his brow. "I don't understand."

Darshana walked over and put a hand on Loni's shoulder. "I believe Kamal's death and Penny's disappearance have hit Loni hard. Along with Yuki, they were all Loni knew for a while. The four of them were like family. And the loss of family is a major trigger to her emotions."

Loni held up her cup, raising a sarcastic brow. "Nothing a little tea won't fix, of course."

Jae studied her. There was no mistaking the deep sadness in her eyes. Her leg was bouncing a bit, and a small film of sweat blanketed her hairline. Her drug addiction was calling her. The pain of losing Kamal and possibility of losing Penny was causing her to crave a fix.

"And the tea helps?" he asked.

"It has a calming effect," Darshana answered. "It will help with her nerves."

Jae stretched out his shoulders. "Maybe I should drink some."

Darshana held a hand up. "No. You're going to be driving, and the tea will make you sleepy. With the police and the Pishacha out there, you're going to want to be alert and focused."

Jae gave her a nod. "Right."

"I know this is taking its toll on you." Darshana set her teacup on the table. "Your position as the elite means you're a target, and that means there's a chance your own sister may try to attack you."

Jae's gaze dropped to the floor. "She's tried to kill me before. I mean, not directly. She sort of hypnotized Mayhara into believing I was the enemy and had her attack me. I was nearly crushed to death under crimson rock."

Darshana placed the tips of her fingers together. "But you got through to her to stop her. To stop both of them."

"Mayhara tried to kill you?" Loni asked. "And you still—?" Loni snapped her mouth shut and turned away from Jae, burying her face in the steam of her tea.

"My point is," Darshana continued, "you found a way

to get through to Naree. She heard you. And I believe that is going to be the key to getting her back. I'm relying on the strength of that connection."

Jae pressed his lips together and nodded. "So am I."

Darshana put a hand on his arm. "Jae, the gods would not have bestowed this task upon you if you weren't worthy enough to handle it. You must believe it is within you to follow through with our part in this war. I believe in you. You should too."

He breathed in deeply, his eyes locked with hers, as if staring at her long enough would convince him of her words.

She patted his arm, as if to stop him from staring, and then returned to drinking her tea.

"All right." He took out keys from his pocket. "I'm going to check my bike and make sure it's in order for the trip."

Darshana nodded and headed for the counter. Jae figured she needed a tea refill. He grabbed the helmets, casting Loni a second's glance before he exited the house. His concern for her was like a pull in his chest. Like muscle memory from their days on the run. He hoped she could keep grounded and resist any cravings for a fix.

It had only been five seconds since he'd closed the door behind him when it opened again. He turned to find Loni stepping out onto the porch. Her mouth was set in a straight line.

"Loni?" He knew he had to tread lightly around her. Resisting approaching her, Jae tightened his grip on the helmets. "Are you—? What are you doing out here?"

"I needed to see you before you go. Just in case." Her voice cracked on the last word.

"Try not to be pessimistic, Loni."

"How can I not be?" She lowered her gaze. "I'm sorry. I don't mean to be so glum. I'm just… I'm worried about you. I lost the closest person to me, and it devastated me. And maybe you don't feel for me anymore what I thought you felt, but I still hold you as one of the most important people in my life. The thought of possibly losing you…"

Tears spilled over and trailed down her cheeks. Her lips trembled and her hands were clenched at her sides.

Jae set the helmets down on the porch and pulled Loni into his arms, unable to stop himself. "Believe me, Loni, I will do everything in my power to keep that from happening."

He felt her nod against his chest, and he kept his arms around her as she wept. He believed she needed this, though he could hear Yuki's warning playing over and over in his mind.

Loni squeezed him tightly, her sniffles disappearing into his jacket.

Just give her another minute, he said to himself.

Right as he was about to let go of her, the door opened once more. His eyes widened when Mayhara stepped out. He knew that when he took a step back from Loni, it must have appeared as though it was because of Mayhara's presence. He didn't want either of them to think that.

Loni looked between Jae and Mayhara as she swiped at her cheeks and cleared her throat.

"Um. Good luck, then," was all she said before heading back into the house.

Mayhara zipped up her leather jacket and tightened the scarf at her neck as she walked past Jae.

A dozen things to say flew though his mind, but he knew every single one of them was wrong. Maybe they'd get a chance to talk during their trip. They'd be on the road for a while, so he'd have plenty of time to think of the proper things to say to her. But for now, all he could think of was, "Ready to go?"

Mayhara adjusted the straps of the backpack she carried. "Yeah. I've got the scroll and Karina's interpretations of the symbols. Plus drinks and food for the road."

"I've got some provisions too. Hopefully, we won't have to stop too often for gas."

He bent down and grabbed the helmets then handed her one. As she took it, he watched her face. He wanted so much to clear the air before they got on his bike, but he knew she would tell him that it wasn't the time. He'd have to find the proper time to do it, if the gods allowed.

⸎

They were making good time up until they were four hours into their journey. Jae spotted a roadblock up ahead on the highway. He muttered a curse to himself, remembering that his face was plastered all over the news sites. Both he and Mayhara were wanted by the police. He moved into the slow lane and used his powers so Mayhara could hear him through their helmets and over the sound of the bike and other vehicles.

"Imperial Police up ahead. Can't go back, and there are no exits before the roadblock. I'm going to use my powers to convince them to let us though."

He felt her nod against his back. He figured she wasn't sure if he could hear her or not. Her hands were resting at his sides, and the closer they got to the police who were checking vehicles, the more her hold would tighten.

The car ahead of them advanced, and Jae forced himself to remain calm. His riding gloves hid his glowing palms, and he focused on the police officer's face as he was waved forward.

The Imperial Police officer studied his face through the helmet's visor. "Where are you headed today?"

Jae pushed out his sapphire energy as he spoke. "To the festival in Vadodara. I promised my girl I'd get her there so we can get a better view of the comet."

It might have been his imagination, but it felt as if Mayhara's hold on his waist had tightened even more when he'd said, 'My girl.'

The officer shifted his gaze back and forth between Jae and Mayhara. Jae continued to push out his power to convince the officer he was telling the truth.

"Can I see some identification, please?"

It hadn't sounded like a question. Jae moved his hand closer to the officer. Startled by his movement, the cop reached for his taser pistol but didn't pull it out. Jae had to act fast to keep him from recognizing them.

"We're not the fugitives you're looking for. You're going to wave us through and wish us a pleasant day."

For a moment, Jae began to panic. The officer hadn't reacted right away. Was the comet blocking his power already? Jae swallowed hard and waited, internally counting the seconds.

The officer took his hand away from his weapon and waved them through. "Have a pleasant day."

Jae gripped the handlebars and nodded his thanks.

It wasn't until they were miles away that he felt Mayhara's hands relax on his waist.

Seven

Shiro wandered the grounds around the house, contemplating a place to hide his dagger. He wasn't sure if the other elites were sticking to the property or venturing outside of the area. And he wasn't supposed to ask.

Movement near the house caught his attention. As Karina lifted her arms, chanting with her eyes closed, Shiro tucked the dagger into the back hem of his jeans and began walking toward her. He made a point of keeping quiet, but his trek was through high grass and dead leaves.

Karina lowered her hands and stopped changing. When she opened her eyes, she focused on Shiro.

"Sorry," he said. "I didn't mean to interrupt."

"No, it's fine." Karina offered him a small smile. "I was finished anyway."

"What were you doing? If you don't mind me asking."

"Darshana asked me to put a protection spell on the house."

"You can do that?"

She let out a small laugh. "I can't attest to the level of my skills, but it's worth a try. I guess I can't be sure if the spell works or not. I did one on our place in the swamp, but my grandmother was attacked outside of our territory, so… it's likely."

"How is she doing?"

Karina bit her lip and shook her head. "It doesn't look good. And when I try to focus on thinking positive, my heart hurts, like it knows it's a lie."

"I've been meaning to see her. I could try another syphoning therapy."

She gave a half-shrug. "I don't know if they're helping. But let's go see if she's awake and ask her. I'm willing to give it another try if she is."

"Yes, let's do that." He held out his arm, gesturing toward the house.

With a nod, she turned toward the house and led the way.

The house was quiet, and Shiro wondered if the other mages were trying to figure out where to hide their daggers. Jae and Mayhara had left earlier that day, but he hadn't really seen much of Yuki, Loni, or Salina.

His thoughts were cut short when Karina opened the door to her room and the sound of Amalia's ragged breathing reached his ears. He felt his heart plummet to his gut, sending a wave of acid surging into his stomach.

Amalia was so pale, her skin appeared gray. Her hair was dry and brittle. Shiro was sure it would crack and break off if it were to be touched. She had lost almost all color in her eyes, leaving them looking like glass. Every small movement she made was done with uncontrollable shaking. And she'd lost a lot of weight, her bones prominent in her arms and fingers.

Shiro came closer, his sympathy riddled with fear. Karina, who sat by her grandmother's side, glanced up at him as she sopped up the sweat from Amalia's forehead with a cloth. He gave Karina a nod, wanting her to be the one to bring up the syphoning therapy.

Karina faced her grandmother and tilted her head. "Do you need anything, Grandmother?"

Amalia's trembling hand clasped on to Karina's. "Just your company, dear."

Karina squeezed her hand. "Shiro is here because we wondered if you need him to get more of the poison out."

Amalia gave her a strained smile, tears pooling in her eyes. "No. It won't do any good."

Shiro took another step forward. "But your pain—"

"I've been speaking with my ancestors," Amalia said. "I am not worried about my pain."

"Grandmother?" Karina's voice was a whisper.

"What does that mean?" Shiro asked. "Speaking with your ancestors?"

"Some witches gain this ability to speak with members of their coven who have passed on. Especially witches closer to death."

Karina's head dropped, her grasp still tight around Amalia's hand.

"It's not important anymore. My suffering." Amalia licked her dry lips. "There is a scroll."

Shiro furrowed his brows. "You mean the one with the cryptic map?"

"No. Another. It is hidden in the spine of the grimoire. I believe this is the scroll Darshana has been having visions of."

The gears in Shiro's brain began turning. "What does the scroll contain?"

"It's a spell the Pishacha never want you to find." Amalia gave Shiro one solid nod. "A spell that can destroy Kashmeru for good."

Shiro held her gaze, his breath catching in his throat. There was a spell to kill Kashmeru. This was the key. The way to end the war. To win the war. To save the world. "It's in the grimoire? The same grimoire that contains the spell to release Kashmeru from his tomb?"

Amalia nodded. "The same. It's a failsafe."

"Why wasn't it used on him before?"

Karina lifted her head, her brows drawn down.

"Because they're connected."

Shiro blanched. "You mean… the Lotus."

Amalia glanced between Karina and Shiro. "Yes. They are linked. It is very likely that killing Kashmeru would also mean the demise of Lakshmi."

A million thoughts tore through Shiro's mind. Jae and Mayhara were on their way to find the grimoire. He needed to text them to let them know about the second, hidden scroll. Though part of him was afraid to tell him the part about the possibility that the spell could kill Jae's sister.

His thoughts were cut short when Yuki suddenly entered the room.

"Yuki?" he asked. "What's wrong?"

Yuki put her hands together. "I'm sorry to interrupt, but there's been a development."

Shiro's heart stopped for a moment, and he feared that something had happened to Jae or Mayhara. Or both.

"It's the extremists." Yuki grabbed her hair and quickly pulled it into a ponytail. "There was a news bulletin about an attack on the New Jaipur City Development Authority Office. I checked the location against the director's scroll that tracks the rebellious activity. They're on the move, but if we hurry, we might be able to catch them."

It took a second for Shiro to wrap his head around this information. This was his chance to talk to Qiang and ask him about the prison camps. He turned toward Karina and Amalia. Karina gave him an understanding smile.

"Yeah." Shiro turned back to face Yuki, his heart thumping in his chest. "Yeah. Let's go find them."

Eight

Penny had waited alone in the basement for Naree and Bhutano to return. Hours must have passed, and she was sure it was the next morning. A part of her held on to the hope that the other elites would be doing what they could to find her. But they had no clue where to start looking. Penny didn't even know where she was.

She'd been left with Daiki—the dark mage with the cheek scar—and another mage whom Daiki called

"Rikuto." While Daiki sat across from Penny, giving her nonstop menacing sneers, Rikuto seemed bored, occupying himself by continuously bending and unbending the blade of a double-edged *tantō*. She knew one of the dark mages was able to manipulate metal, and Rikuto proved to be him. His hair was buzzed short on the sides, with the rest pulled into a ponytail. He wore a long, dark gray cloak over a loose, white, button-down shirt. And there was a prominent tattoo on his neck, a symbol Penny didn't recognize.

She wondered if so much bending and unbending was damaging the *tantō* at all. She couldn't imagine the blade upholding its sturdiness and being useful after so much manipulating.

"Hey, Penny," Daiki called. The smirk on his face made her cringe.

"What?"

"Are you afraid of scorpions?"

She shot him a questioning look, noticing his gaze falling to her knee. She flinched when she found a scorpion there, crawling up her leg into her lap. She held back a scream, but small sounds of panic emerged from her throat as the scorpion crept along.

Suddenly, the door opened. Naree and Bhutano strode in, their faces stoic.

Penny glanced back down at her leg, her forehead wrinkling when she found the scorpion gone. Had it crawled under the chair? Had it managed to get inside her clothing? She tried not to squirm so as not to anger it if it was near her skin.

"I hope this time we've given you has provided a moment for you to think," Bhutano said, checking his watch. "You simply have to cooperate with us, and no harm will come to you."

Naree seemed to glide through the room. She looked rested, as if she'd gotten some sleep. Her hair was like silk, and her skin was glowing. She didn't seem like a prisoner, like she was being controlled by an evil god. She looked as though she was being pampered and cared for. But Penny knew it was all a ruse. Kashmeru was controlling her, making her believe that her life was better with him, convincing her that this was where she was supposed to be by showing her how good life was in his world. But the truth was she was being held in a golden cage, trapped in deceitful beauty, with no freedom of her own.

"Like I said before," Penny said to him, "I don't know where the daggers are. And they're not easy to track down."

"But this time, it will be different," Naree said, settling into the chair across from her. "We can search for them together. With the influence of my powers and your connection to the other elites, it should be easier than when you had to do it before."

The wheels in Penny's head were spinning as she desperately tried to find a way to keep Naree from seeing the daggers. If she could even find them with her mind. "Fine. I can't do it like this, though."

"What do you mean?" Naree asked.

"I need my hands free."

Daiki moved forward, his fists resting on his waist. "Aren't they?"

Penny almost scoffed. "They're bound in these electro-cuffs."

Daiki smirked. "What electro-cuffs?"

Penny furrowed a brow and moved her hands. They didn't meet any resistance, and she stared in wonder at her wrists as she brought her hands in front of her face.

"How did—?"

From the back of the room, Penny heard a low chuckle. Bhutano pushed himself off the wall where he was leaning and straightened the cuffs of his Imperial Police uniform. "I see you've got things under control, Your Highness. I'll leave you to it. I've got something else Kashmeru wants me to take care of for now, but I'll be back to check on your progress."

Bhutano locked eyes with Penny as he left the room, his gait full of self-confidence.

Penny's gaze went back to Daiki, who was still smirking at her.

Naree shifted in her chair. "Daiki has the power to manipulate your thoughts. You only believed you were cuffed because he made you think it was so."

Penny scratched her tongue with her teeth as she took in this information. That explained the scorpion. He'd only made her believe there was one, but it had been an illusion. These mages had powers she hadn't known existed. Not knowing what you were up against made things much scarier to deal with. She really needed to watch her step.

She glanced around at the other dark mages, and Naree followed her gaze.

"I suppose you're curious about the other soldiers," Naree said, "and what they might be able to do."

Penny kept her mouth in a straight line, not wanting to answer but curious still.

Naree crossed her legs and leaned back in the chair. She pointed to Rikuto, the one who'd been bending and unbending the *tantō*. "That's Rikuto. An orphan, like you. He has the power to manipulate metal."

Rikuto stuffed his hands in the pockets of his dark gray cloak and stretched out his neck. Penny got a glimpse of his neck tattoo, noting that it matched the one on Director Shei's daughter.

"The bald one in the corner is Kun," Naree said, gesturing in his direction with her chin. "He's got a very special power. Able to sicken his victims, even to the point of infecting them with poison."

Kun had a thin face, almost skeletal. His eyes were as black as coal, and dark circles lurked beneath them. He too had a tattoo on his neck. Penny wondered if they all had the tattoo and she'd just never noticed it.

"Then, of course, we have Harish." Naree nodded to him. "Son of the wealthiest family in New Jaipur, and a syphoner. He can drain energy of any kind, whether it be electrical, mechanical, human, or magical. And our little lady by the table is Ruolan Shei, daughter of the government's census director. I'd love to tell you she has a beautiful smile, but I'm afraid I've never seen it. Ru can move things by pulling and pushing energy. A telekinetic, if you will."

"The quiet one over there," Naree said, pointing to the dark-skinned young man with short brown hair, "that's Jin-woo, and he's got a special talent. He can manipulate the slithery things of this world. Insects, snakes, weeds, vines… things of that nature."

Jin-woo had a beautiful face, almost feminine. Perhaps that was why he'd shaved lines into his eyebrows, to give him a more edgy look. Jin-woo held up a hand, which emanated black tendrils of smoke that made their way toward Penny. The tendrils turned into creeping vines, sliding along the floor as if they were snakes and finding Penny's legs. The vines circled her legs and wrapped themselves around them until she was bound.

Daiki let out a laugh. "Now you really are tied up."

Naree looked over her other shoulder. "And of course, there's Avi: the bone crusher. I believe some of your colleagues are familiar with him."

Penny looked away from him, not wanting him to see her fear.

Naree leaned forward, her arm draped over her knee. "Together, they make up the Council of the Seven. Kashmeru has gifted these special talents to them, chosen them to be the powerful assets in his shadow army. You see what you are up against, and that doesn't even put a dent in what I can do to you." Naree studied her. "Are you ready to cooperate now?"

Penny chewed at her lip as she weighed her options. "It might not work, you know?"

"It's totally worth a try, though. Isn't it?" Naree flashed her a wicked smile.

Penny's heart thrummed in her chest. She knew there was no way out of this situation, but that didn't mean she had to play entirely by the enemy's rules. After all, meditation was a way for her to reach out with her mind.

Who was to say that she wouldn't *accidentally* reach out to Darshana?

Penny nodded. "Fine."

"Good," Naree said. "Let's begin."

Penny took a deep breath, concentrating on breathing slowly. She cleared her mind, erasing thoughts of electro-cuffs and scorpions and bendable *tantōs*. She listened to her breaths and relaxed her shoulders, her arms, her hands.

"Good," Naree said in a gentle voice. "Now picture the daggers. Picture the blade, the hilt, the design. Pull that picture of it up in your mind. Search for it."

Penny thought of Darshana. Her kind smile. Her wise words. The motherly way about her.

Her eyes came into focus in her mind.

"What are you doing?" Naree asked, seeing what Penny saw.

"I'm looking for the daggers."

"But that's your guru in your head."

"Maybe she's near them." Penny hoped Naree would buy her excuse.

Darshana. Can you hear me?

Instead of an answer, Penny's mind zoomed out to see

Darshana handing Mr. Kitaro a box.

"What was that?" Naree's voice was sharp.

Penny opened her eyes to find Naree glaring at her. "I don't know."

"Don't lie to me."

Naree raised one of her hands. Avi stepped forward with a sneer on his face. Black tendrils of smoke swirled through the air. A shooting pain erupted in Penny's pinky finger. She bent forward and cried out in pain, feeling the slicing burn of her bone being crushed.

Penny gasped. "I'm not lying. I swear. I don't know what that was." As tears came to her eyes, she tried to breathe through the pain.

"Don't you see that that was totally unnecessary?" Naree asked. She clicked her tongue a few times. "If you'd just stay the course, we could have avoided that."

Penny bit back a whimper. Her eyes flit over Naree's face, confused at how she could have turned out this way.

"Why are you letting him control you?" Penny asked.

Naree blanched, not having expected the question.

"Can't you see he's poisoning you?" Penny placed her hand in her lap and tried not to think about her pain. "The longer you stay under the spell, the more you lose yourself."

"You wouldn't understand. Our love, our fate, the pull between us…These are things that have existed for centuries, so I wouldn't expect a mere mortal to truly wrap their simple mind around it." Naree took a deep breath and let it out. "He loves me."

"Kashmeru has a twisted idea of love, Your Highness."

Naree's lips pressed into a slash. She clenched her jaw and stretched out her neck. "You know, I don't believe you've ever been in love. You wouldn't know the lengths one would go to for you, or you for them. You wouldn't understand sacrifices and compromises. And you certainly wouldn't understand the feeling when someone you're meant to be with holds you and promises you the world."

"Naree." Penny tried a different approach. "Lakshmi. You're pure good. You represent all that's right in the world. You know Kashmeru is evil. You have to break free from his hold on you."

Avi stepped forward again. "I think that's enough out of you. Unless you want another little taste of my special medicine."

Penny could feel her finger throbbing. She dropped her gaze, unwilling to face more pain.

"Here." Naree reached into her trouser pocket and pulled out a tiny, carved, jade dragonfly. She admired it for a moment, turning it between her fingers. "Maybe this will help you get a better connection. Jae gave this to me."

"And you still have it," Penny remarked. "It must mean something to you."

Hope bloomed in her chest at the realization that Naree was still holding Jae near to her heart. She was sure she saw something there in Naree's eyes when she was gazing at it. Maybe there was still a chance to get through to her.

Naree looked up at her and scowled. "It serves only as a connection to him so that I can reach him and convince him to give up his fight. Perhaps it will serve as a connection for you to find him and the location of the daggers." Naree placed it in Penny's hand. "Try again."

Penny frowned. She didn't know how to get through to Naree and free her from Kashmeru. And now she herself was being forced to work for their side. Her stomach roiled and her chest felt as if it were caving in on itself.

Penny cleared her mind again. She felt the cool surface of the jade dragonfly between her fingers. It began to warm in her hand, and her mind was drawn to it. Suddenly, Jae's eyes appeared before her in her mind. It was as if a camera were zoomed in on his face, the focus smudged around the edges. Her mind's eye zoomed out slowly, and she could see Jae speaking to Mayhara. They were near his motorcycle. She couldn't make out the words. Jae was filling the bike with gas, and Mayhara was checking her backpack. She pulled out a scroll.

Penny snapped her mind shut, not wanting Naree to see. The jade dragonfly slipped from her fingers and fell to the floor. When she opened her eyes, she could tell it was too late. Naree had seen what she'd seen. She hadn't meant to show her the image, but her mind had gone right to Jae when she'd held the dragonfly.

Naree smiled. "Now we're getting somewhere."

Nine

By the time Shiro and Yuki got to the New Jaipur City Development Authority Office, the only traces of the extremist group to be found were the scattered rubble and the smoke still wafting in the air from the explosion they'd set off in the building. Shiro looked around at the damage Qiang and his gang had done in their attempt to strike back at the government for making mages illegal. He shook his head, still in disbelief of the lengths Qiang would go to. This was the same man who'd taken care of him in the prison camps. The same man who'd cried in his arms when the life of one of their own had been brutally taken by prison guards. Shiro never would have imagined that the kind, gentle man he'd fallen in love with would be able to cause so much death and destruction.

Shiro scanned the area. There was a cleanup crew tending to the area, but it seemed like most of the police had cleared out along with the fire department and the medics.

"Any idea of where they went?" Shiro asked.

"The scroll will only show where the extremists attacked. The lights eventually fade after the event ends." Yuki checked her Linq. "I don't see any more reports on the news sites, but I'm going to check the Spottit app. They have a sub-thread for people who've witnessed riots or protests and stuff. Maybe someone saw something after the extremists took off, and we can get a lead."

As Yuki scrolled through the app, Shiro checked to make sure the four Imperial Police officers patrolling the area didn't recognize them. Especially Yuki, since her picture had just been up on the recent new bulletins. He hoped the officers were too preoccupied with the aftermath of the attack.

"Okay, got it." Yuki's eyes widened. "Someone spotted them entering an abandoned building on South Gaoling Street."

"That's this way." Shiro gestured as he briskly walked toward the street in question.

It took some maneuvering to avoid the police, but eventually, they reached South Gaoling Street. A few old shops were scattered along the street, with very few patrons. The place looked like it had been hit hard by recession. Trash spilled out from receptacles along the sidewalks, and mud caked the gutters. It seemed a likely place for the extremist group to lie low. It was just a matter of finding the abandoned building they were in.

Shiro glanced in windows as they made their way down the street. Yuki's hands were closed into fists, but Shiro could just make out the faint white glow she was trying to conceal.

Yuki hissed through her teeth. "Feeling some strange hostility up ahead."

"Okay. It's probably that theater. I think it's been closed for a couple of years now, and it looks big enough to hold a group like Qiang's."

They picked up their pace, not wanting to miss their opportunity to catch Qiang. Shiro checked over his shoulder as they made their way to the entrance. For a moment, he became paranoid that someone might post about them on the Spottit app.

The sound of Yuki jiggling the door handle snapped Shiro from his thoughts.

"It's locked," she said. "Maybe if we go arou—"

Suddenly, he felt as if the world were turning upside-down. It wasn't until he landed on his arm—and Yuki landed on her back next to him—that he realized someone had used crimson powers on them.

Shiro and Yuki called upon their powers, their palms glowing as they shifted to stand.

"I wouldn't do that if I were you." The woman who spoke hovered above them, glaring. Her glowing red palms were aimed in their direction. Her hair was short and spiky, and her sleeveless top exposed her lean muscles.

A large, dark-skinned man appeared at her side.

"What are we going to do with these two, Kyoko?"

"Let's get them inside before someone sees." Kyoko lowered her hands.

The big man bent down and grabbed Shiro and Yuki by their shirts, lifting them to their feet.

"Wait." Shiro held up his hands in surrender. "We're here to see Qiang."

"Keep it down," Kyoko snapped. She eyed her partner. "We can put them in the back, Rajim."

"You think they really know Qiang?" Rajim asked.

Kyoko scoffed as she led the way to a side door. "Doubt it."

Shiro flinched as Rajim shoved him through the door. "I do know Qiang. We're close, personal friends."

"Funny." Kyoko looked him up and down. "I've never seen you around."

Shiro glanced at Yuki.

"It's okay," she said in a soft voice. "Stay calm. We'll get this sorted."

He wasn't sure if she was using her powers, but he noticed his heartbeat slowing and his breathing coming easier.

"Listen," Shiro said to Kyoko. "We don't want any trouble. But I need to speak with Qiang."

Kyoko pursed her lips. "Well, Qiang's not here right now. And I can't very well let you go without knowing your objective, so Rajim and I are just going to have to keep you locked up in the back until he gets back."

Rajim grabbed Yuki's and Shiro's arms and forced them through the theater. Members of Qiang's extremist group gathered in the large room, some sprawled out on the seats, and some grouped together near the stage, checking their weapons. All eyes were on Shiro and Yuki as they were led across the room and through a door.

Rajim pushed them toward a couple of chairs. "Have a seat."

Shiro and Yuki did as they were told.

Kyoko held out glowing red palms and pushed out crimson energy at their feet. Crimson earth sealed their feet to the floor. "Just so you don't get any clever ideas," she said, smirking.

"When will Qiang be back?" Shiro asked.

Kyoko let out a laugh. "I guess we'll just have to wait and see, won't we?"

She hit Rajim's arm with the back of her hand, and the two of them exited the room, locking the door behind them.

Ten

Jae mumbled a curse when the CLOSED ROAD sign appeared ahead. A wide wooden barricade blocked the street, and just beyond it, he could see the tents, lights, and rides of the Vadodara festival. They had just gassed up the motorcycle, and he'd thought they could cut down their travel time by driving through the night. But this threw a wrench in their plans.

He pulled over as the road ended and cut the engine.

Along the sides of the road, dozens of vehicles were parked, some of them in the grass, filling a makeshift parking lot for the festivalgoers.

Mayhara pulled off her helmet. "Looks like the road is closed because of the festival. It's like your lie became a truth."

"We'll need to double back and find an alternate road to Pune. We might have to find a back road, which could unfortunately take longer."

"Mind if I stretch my legs for a minute?" Mayhara asked. "I'm starting to cramp up."

"No, go ahead." Jae dismounted after she did and hooked their helmets to the bike. "I could use some stretching myself."

They paced the side of the road a few yards. Jae noticed that Mayhara seemed to be creating more distance between them, as if she needed to be farther away from him after having held on to him for hours. He let out a sigh and let her wander. He knew she needed time and space; he just wished he were more patient in giving them to her.

Fireworks began going off over their heads. The

sounds of music and chatter from the festival reached his ears between the bursts of light. Jae admired the fireworks display for a minute, caught up in the feeling of sharing the moment with Mayhara—even if she stood more than twenty feet away. He longed to stand beside her and take her hand, but he knew she might pull away and break his heart all over again.

"Jae."

He tore his eyes away from the sky to find Mayhara plodding his way, staring wide-eyed over his shoulder. Following her gaze, he noticed three Imperial Police on foot, patrolling the grounds of the festival and headed their way.

Jae was about to bolt back to his motorcycle when he spotted a patrol car slowly advancing toward them.

At that moment, a van full of teenagers unloaded, the rowdy youngsters whooping and laughing, pointing at the fireworks as they made their way past Jae and Mayhara, heading to the festival.

"Come on," Jae said once Mayhara was near enough. "Blend in."

He took her hand and led her toward the barrier. They

caught up with the group of teenagers and walked in close enough proximity that it could appear they were part of the entourage. Mayhara glanced over her shoulder at the Imperial Police as she lifted her scarf to cover her hair.

"We're going to have to wait until they're gone before we can risk going back to the bike." Jae gave her a reassuring nod.

She nodded back, visibly swallowing.

As they reached the throng of festivalgoers, Jae spotted a hat that had fallen onto the ground near a novelty stand. Without stopping, he stooped down to pick it up and placed it on his head, sparing a glance behind him.

"There are police everywhere," he whispered close to Mayhara's ear. "I feel like we just waltzed into the lion's den."

Mayhara scanned the crowd, confirming his words. "How are we going to get out of here?"

"I'm not sure." Jae looked around, examining the surrounding buildings on the outskirts of the festival. "Let's find a place to lie low until we can figure out how to evade them."

She gave him a nod. Jae still had her hand in his as he

led her through the crowd. He kept his head ducked to avoid getting noticed by the police or anyone else who might recognize him from the news bulletin.

As he glanced at an officer standing near a sweet bun stand, panic shot through him. The officer had noticed him and was following his movements. Jae wasn't sure if he'd recognized him or if he was just curious. Trying not to seem too obvious, Jae picked up his pace. As they got closer to one building, he noticed a worker in uniform exit the basement entrance of a shop. The worker carried a large box that mostly obstructed his view. With his arms full, the worker attempted to close the door behind himself by kicking it. He continued up the stairs and on his way, and Jae noticed the ground shift at the doorway. Crimson earth had formed a doorstop, keeping the door from fully closing.

Jae turned to Mayhara, whose hand was raised, the faint glow of red fading from her palm.

"Good catch," he said.

"Thanks. Let's go."

He checked once more to make sure they weren't being watched. The officer who had spotted him before was no longer at his station. Jae wasn't sure if he'd followed them, so he picked up speed. Jae and Mayhara descended the stairs together quickly and slipped into the basement door. Mayhara waved her hand, and the crimson doorstop disintegrated.

It was dark inside the basement room, but festival lights shone through a narrow window that had a view of the street, giving them enough illumination to see where they were walking. Jae checked out the window, seeing mostly the bottom halves of festivalgoers' legs.

"I don't think anyone followed us, but I can't be sure." He turned back to Mayhara, who was lowering her scarf from her head. "I want to give that officer a little time to forget he saw us."

Mayhara let out a sigh. "Yeah. Sounds good. Otherwise, we'll have to stay here until the festival is over."

"These things tend to go until dawn. I don't think we want to wait that long."

Jae watched her as she came to stand beside him at the window. His eyes traveled over the curve of her cheek, the plumpness of her lips. Her nearness stirred up the urge inside him to talk to her.

"Mayhara, I know this probably isn't the right time—
"

"No. It isn't."

Jae let out a slow breath. "I've got the feeling we're going to be short of right times, given the situation."

She crossed her arms over her chest and took a step back, but she didn't turn away from him. "What is it?"

His heart thrummed in his chest. His mind scrambled for the words as he internally reminded himself that he was a sapphire mage, the very mage who ruled the throat chakra, and he should be a master of communication.

"I don't want there to be any bad feelings between us. I hate that you can't even look at me without hate in your eyes. I'm sorry for not telling you about Loni, and I wasn't taking her side over yours. I was just trying to stop the fighting and keep things from escalating."

Mayhara searched his face. "I don't hate you, Jae. I could never."

Partial relief bloomed in his heart. "My feelings for you haven't changed. You've got to know that."

She narrowed her eyes. "Really? Because you seemed awfully chummy with Loni on the front porch this morning."

"No. No, that was nothing. She's in a bad place and I was offering comfort. As a *friend*."

She bit her cheek, her brows drawn down. "I don't think she sees it that way."

"I… I know. But I can't be responsible for how she feels. I can only be responsible for how I feel."

She seemed confused as she blinked, rubbing her arms. They were both quiet for a long moment, and Jae felt his hope plummet.

"I understand that you feel we can't be as close as we were before, but I would be devastated if our friendship was unsalvageable."

She tucked a strand of hair behind her ear. "It's not… unsalvageable."

"It's not?"

"Of course not." Her voice was a whisper.

He kept his gaze on her a moment longer. A noise outside the window caught their attention. Four pair of legs in Imperial Police uniforms marched by the window. Jae and Mayhara backed up, ducking out of sight.

"We need a distraction," Jae said.

Mayhara's palm lit up, and she held the red light closer to some boxes on a shelf. "This could work."

Jae came closer and read the labels on the boxes. "Fireworks?"

"Fire*crackers*. The kind that go off on the ground and make a lot of noise. If we set one off in the alley where no one is, it could distract the police, and we could make a break for it."

He nodded. "Okay. Yeah, that could work."

Jae grabbed a box off the shelf while Mayhara checked the window.

"Okay, no sign of the police." Mayhara went toward the door. "Get ready."

With Mayhara leading the way, they climbed the stairs and headed for the alley. It was a long corridor and—as luck would have it—totally vacant.

"There," Mayhara said. "Behind the dumpster."

As they raced down the alley toward the dumpster, Mayhara pulled her scarf over her hair. She and Jae crouched near the side of the dumpster, and Jae set the box down.

"This is a big box," Jae said. "It's going to cause quite

a racket."

"Just what we need."

As Mayhara created a small glow to give them some light, Jae pushed the button on the electro-lighter and held it to the corner of the box. As soon as the flame caught, Jae dropped the lighter and pulled Mayhara to stand.

"Let's go."

Their hands were still joined as they hurried out of the alley and pushed their way through the crowd. Jae checked left and right as they zigzagged through the throng of people. A couple of Imperial Police noticed them, giving curious looks, but the moment one of them began to move their way, the loud, tumultuous popping and clattering of firecrackers echoed throughout the air. The noises made everyone flinch. The police wasted no time rushing to find the source. Many people in the crowd screamed, mistaking the noise for gunfire. Some panicked and fled away from the offensive racket.

Jae welcomed the surge of people running from the festival, using the opportunity to mix with the crowd and get to his bike. If anything, any suspicious police would find the swarm of panicked citizens an obstacle. He just had to make sure not to let go of Mayhara's hand.

The crowd spread out as they reached the barricade on the road that separated the festival from the street. Jae and Mayhara checked behind them as they sprinted to Jae's bike. Jae unhooked Mayhara's helmet and handed it to her.

But the second he picked up his helmet, a voice materialized in his head.

Jae.

He froze at the sound of Naree's voice. Shock pushed through him, and he had to turn around and scan the crowd to make sure she wasn't actually there.

"What is it?" Mayhara asked.

He was about to answer when he heard his sister's voice again.

I see you. You shouldn't run. It's of no use. I will find you.

Jae wasn't sure if he should answer. His heart wanted to reason with her, to tell her to come to him so he could rescue her from the evil god controlling her. Instead, he turned to Mayhara. They needed to get to the grimoire before the Pishacha did. He just hoped Naree didn't know that that was where they were headed.

"We've got to go," he said to Mayhara. "She's going to catch on to our plan."

A wrinkle formed on Mayhara's forehead. "Who?"

"Naree. She's talking to me in my head. She's trying to stop us. We don't have any time to lose."

"Yeah. Okay." Mayhara seemed to fight off a shiver. She shoved the helmet on and nodded. "Let's go."

Jae mounted the bike, still glancing around to convince himself Naree wasn't there, that there wouldn't suddenly be an army of Pishacha ready to jump them. He started the motorcycle, and as soon as Mayhara's hands were around his waist, he drove off.

Eleven

Karina took the teacup from Amalia's trembling hands. They didn't have access to the special herbs Amalia usually used in her teas, but Darshana had made her a brew that was supposed to keep her more comfortable.

"Any better, Grandmother?"

"I'm pretty sure it has valerian root, which means I'll get tired rather quickly."

Karina stroked her arm. "That's okay. You need to rest."

"But we still need to talk, dear."

"Grandmother, we can talk later."

Amalia reached for her hand. "No. We might not get a chance, and I have a lot to tell you. We should speak now."

A shiver traveled up and down Karina's spine, but she resisted shaking it off.

"What did you want to talk about?" Karina feared she knew the answer, but she wasn't sure she was ready for it.

Amalia shifted, and Karina immediately helped her by fixing her pillows to prop her up.

"Your mother passed away when you were a baby, so you wouldn't remember what happens at a witch's funeral, what needs to be done."

Karina wrung her hands. "I… Do we have to talk about funerals?"

"I think we do. And it's important for you to know. And it's relevant for what could be your part in the prophecy."

"My part?" She inched closer.

"A very powerful witch is need for the spells involved with the prophecy. The Pishacha need a powerful witch to release Kashmeru from his tomb, and the Empire needs one to destroy him."

"You think the Pishacha have a powerful witch?"

Amalia shook her head slowly. "I don't know."

"And you think the Empire will need me to destroy Kashmeru?"

"You are already at their disposal. But beyond that, I believe fate has handed you to them."

Karina bit her lip. "I don't know if I'm that powerful. I wasn't even sure I cast the protection spell on the house properly."

Amalia patted her hand. "You come from a long line of powerful witches. It's in your blood. But what I'm about to tell you in regards to my death—and my funeral—will ensure that you are powerful enough when the time comes."

Karina furrowed her brow, bracing herself. "Okay. What is it?"

"When a witch dies, it's important she is returned to the earth. Witches are devoted to nature, and we are put back to the place from whence we came. Given our situation, I will have to be buried on Mr. Kitaro's property. So it's important that you consecrate the ground in which you'll lay my body."

Karina squirmed in her chair as she nodded. She wasn't ready to face the fact that her grandmother would die soon, but she knew these details were important.

"Now here's the vital part," Amalia continued. "My powers will be buried with me and flow into the earth, but you can perform a ritual to transfer that power to you."

Karina's head was spinning. "What does the ritual involve?"

"I will teach you the incantation you need to recite. But to increase its effectiveness, you'll need help from the mages. Even one mage can help with the potency of the spell, but all seven would push its power to the fullest. I truly hope Penny is found and rescued when the time comes, but if not, the other six will do."

"What do the mages have to do?"

"Each mage must generate energy particles from their powers, and these particles must be strewn over my grave while you recite the incantation. The particles will then dissolve into my grave, drawing out my power. This power will then flow to you and become yours, making you one of the most—if not *the* most—powerful witch in New United Asia."

Karina looked at her hands. There was a tenseness in the pit of her stomach that caused her to bite the inside of her cheek. "I understand."

"I'm not saying your destiny is to unlock Kashmeru's tomb. Perhaps the Pishacha have a witch to carry out that part. But should you have the chance to destroy Kashmeru, if it comes to that, you will have the power within you to carry through with it."

Karina locked eyes with her grandmother for what seemed like forever. Amalia breathed in a ragged breath and began letting out a barrage of coughs. Karina scooted closer and rubbed her back, her face contorted in worry.

As Amalia's coughs faded, she waved off Karina. "It's important for you to understand that, because of this power, the Pishacha will be after you. They will know you can open the tomb, and they will do anything they can to get their hands on you."

Karina took her hand and held it to her chest. "I'll be

careful. I promise.”

Amalia stroked her cheek. “I love you, Karina.”

“I love you, too, grandmother.”

Amalia smiled, and for a moment, Karina didn’t see any pain in her face.

“Now, dear,” Amalia said as she patted Karina’s hand, “that valerian root is kicking in. So if you don’t mind—”

“Oh! Yes, of course.” Karina adjusted the pillows. “Get some rest. I’ll check on you later.”

“I’ll teach you the incantation after my nap.”

“All right.”

As Karina fixed the bedsheets, Amalia closed her eyes. By the time Karina left the room, Amalia had fallen asleep.

When Karina made it to the main room, she found Darshana, Loni, and Salina sitting cross-legged on the rug. Darshana’s eyes were closed, but Loni and Salina had their eyes open. Karina’s brows sunk down, and she aimed a questioning look at them. Loni held a finger to her lips to signal to her to keep quiet. Salina gestured to Darshana with her head and then placed her fingers on her temples. Karina understood the message and sat quietly on the couch to wait for Darshana to finish meditating.

"You're not as quiet as you think you are," Darshana said, her eyes still closed.

Loni and Salina whispered their apologies.

Darshana opened her eyes and let out a sigh as she uncrossed her legs and stood. "It's no use."

"You can't find her?" Salina asked.

"I see glimpses of her. I know she's trying to figure out how to get out of the Pishacha's grasp. But I don't know where she is. It's as if the signal is blocked, or as if there is a thick glass standing in the way between us. Something is interrupting the telepathic bond."

Loni looked between Darshana and Salina. "So what do we do?"

Karina inched forward on the couch. "Maybe I can help."

Loni raised her brows. "How?"

"I don't know what magic the Pishacha are using to keep her location concealed, but I could try to do a locator spell."

Salina sat up straighter. "It's worth a try, right?"

"Yeah." Loni nodded. "Let's do it."

"What do you need?" Darshana asked.

"I need something of Penny's. Something personal with meaning. The more meaning, the better. I also need a paper map. A map of New United Asia is probably best, since we're not sure how far the Pishacha may have taken her. And I need a knife."

Loni and Salina stood.

"I think I know what personal object might work," Loni said. "I'll go get it from our room."

"I will ask Mr. Kitaro for a map," Darshana said. "I have a feeling he will have one."

"And I guess I'll get the knife," Salina said. "What are we talking? Steak knife? Butter knife?"

Karina smiled at her. "I need it to slice my palm, so it's going to have to be sharper than a butter knife."

Salina grimaced. "Gotcha."

Salina was the first to return, seeing as the kitchen wasn't far from the main room.

A few moments later, Loni showed up holding a necklace. "This was her mother's. Her parents passed away after a car accident. Of all the things Penny kept after their death, this is the only thing she still has. The rest was lost or destroyed during the Eradication."

Karina held her hand out to take it. "That'll work."

Darshana entered the room. Not only did she have a map with her, but she was also accompanied by Mr. Kitaro. "One map of New United Asia. Though, from the looks of it, it was before some of the border changes."

"It should still work," Karina said as she took the map and lay it on the floor.

Kneeling so that the map was in front of her, Karina held the knife in her left hand and swiped the blade across the palm of her right hand. She then placed her palm on the map, in their current location, and began moving her hand in a circular motion. Blood smeared along the map as she continued to move her hand, the circles she formed growing bigger until she'd covered the map in her blood. As she recited the chant she had learned when she'd been younger, she held Penny's necklace in her bloody hand and closed her eyes. She imagined Penny's face as she repeated the chant.

"Whoa," she heard Loni say.

Karina opened her eyes. On the map, the city of Agra stood out, cleared of Karina's blood.

"That's where she is?" Salina asked.

"Looks that way." Karina set Penny's necklace down. "Though it's a lot of ground to cover."

Loni began pacing. "Okay, I say Salina and I head to Agra. I think it's a four-hour drive. In the meantime, maybe you guys can get a hold of a detailed map of that city. Karina, will the locator spell work if you did it again on that map?"

"Yes, it should."

"And then we'll have the location narrowed down some more." Loni looked expectantly at Karina, hope in her eyes.

"Yeah. We can linq you the location once we've figured it out."

Salina rubbed her hands together. "Perfect. I'll get my jacket."

"Me too." Loni pointed at Mr. Kitaro. "Can you get the map of Agra?"

Mr. Kitaro nodded. "Yes. No problem."

Loni and Salina swept out of the room to prepare for their trip. Karina went to the kitchen to wash the blood off her hands and the necklace. She took a deep breath and let it out slowly, hoping she had helped. Her mind moved to her grandmother's words about gaining more power, and a chill rushed through her at the thought of being able to carry out magic more powerful than a simple locator spell. It was exciting but terrifying, especially when it came to the fate of the world.

She turned to Darshana, who was folding up Mr. Kitaro's map. She could see the worry in her expression and hoped that Loni and Salina would find Penny before it was too late.

Twelve

Naree stepped into the kitchen just as one of the staff had finished making her tea. She needed a short break from using her powers on Penny. She hadn't imagined it would be so difficult to break her so they could find the daggers. Sipping her tea, she told herself not to give up. Progress was slow, but it was still progress.

As she leaned her hip against the counter, something

in the pocket of her slacks pressed hard against her. She set down the teacup and reached into her pocket, pulling out the jade dragonfly. Running her thumb over the smooth, cool surface, she couldn't help but think of Jae and when he'd given it to her.

"Jae, I don't want to go back. Mom and Dad are suffocating me." Naree plopped down on the couch in Jae's tiny apartment and crossed her arms over her chest.

Jae sat next to her on the couch and bumped her with his elbow. "I know. You can stay here for a while. I talked to them, and they finally agreed."

Naree gave him a small smile and rested her head on his shoulder. "Thank you."

"You don't sound so overjoyed."

"Because I know I'll eventually have to go back." Naree sighed. "I know deep down that they are right. That there is something sinister our there just biding its time before it can get to me. And I know they want to protect me from that. But I feel like a prisoner. I haven't even met anyone outside our immediate family, and I don't have any friends."

Jae put his arm around her and squeezed her. "I'm sorry

you're going through this."

"I mean, imagine an entire school of mages dedicated to honoring me, and I can't even attend it. I can't even let any of them know I exist. Do you know how frustrating that is? I have my very own empire, and I'm not even allowed to let anyone know I'm the Lotus."

"Well, I know you are." Jae shifted to face her. "I have a feeling it won't always be like this. Maybe one day, something will change, and you will be able to take your place on the throne and witness your empire with your very own eyes."

The smallest of smiles tugged on her lips. "That would be lovely."

"In the meantime, I can't offer you a throne, but I can give you this as a reminder of adaptability and self-realization."

He pulled a small object out of his jacket pocket and handed it to her.

She gazed upon the small, jade carving of a dragonfly. It represented change.

"This is gorgeous," she said. "Thank you."

"I made it just for you."

"You made this? Wow, that's incredible." She threw her arms around him, pulling him in for a hug. "I know I don't

know a lot of people, but I have to say you are the best brother ever."

He laughed and hugged her in return.

One of the kitchen staff entered the kitchen and spotted her teacup. "Did you need more tea, ma'am?"

Naree slipped the jade dragonfly back into her pocket and tucked a strand of hair behind her ear. "No thank you."

The staff member nodded and headed for the pantry, probably to prepare the next meal.

Lakshmi, my love.

A pang in Naree's chest caused her to hunch over slightly. "Yes?"

The comet is approaching. Do not let me down.

"I won't." She cleared her throat and squared her shoulders. "I promise."

With her chin lifted, she exited the kitchen to head back to the room Penny was being held in. She had a mission, and she was going to keep her promise and see it through.

Thirteen

Penny was exhausted. Though Naree pushed her to concentrate on the daggers, Penny was doing everything she could not to. When Naree would call her out, Penny would lie and tell her the meditation wasn't working. But the truth was she did have a strong connection to the elite mages and her powers, partnered with Naree's, would probably be enough to track them down.

But she couldn't let that happen.

The door to the room opened, and Bhutano walked in. He only spared Penny a glance before directing his focus on Naree.

"Your Highness, are we making any progress?"

She cleared her throat. "Small steps."

"What does that mean?" His eyes darted to Penny for a second before addressing Naree again. "Have you found the daggers or not?"

Naree tightened her jaw.

Bhutano straightened the cuffs of his uniform. "I see. Perhaps she needs a bit more motivation."

Naree averted her gaze and nodded. "Yes, of course."

"I'm certain you can handle this with five of the seven?" he asked. "I have a special assignment for Harish and Daiki."

Naree gave him a slight nod. "I understand."

Penny turned her gaze away from Bhutano.

Naree scooted closer to her. "Do not disappoint me, amethyst mage. Do not forget whom I have at my disposal. Even five of the seven would be too much for you to handle. Now close your eyes and concentrate."

Penny took a deep breath. She didn't want to anger Naree, especially with Bhutano in the room. But she also wanted to hear what special assignment Bhutano had for two of his dark mages. She closed her eyes, pretending to get into the meditative state, but her ears were tuned in to Bhutano's conversation.

"We're ready to move forward with our plan regarding the prison camps." Although he kept his voice to hushed tones, Penny could still make out his words. "I've got Pishacha soldiers setting up detonation devices throughout all the prison camps. Daiki, I need you to change the views of any witnesses so that they believe these devices were set up by the extremists. Harish, you are to find any uprising in the camps and drain the powers of the rebels. Syphon their powers and dispose of them."

Penny swallowed hard. Bhutano meant that he should kill them.

"Take some of the Pishacha soldiers with you," Bhutano continued. "I have to meet with the governor to organize details behind the scenes and finalize our story to the press."

Penny's eyes were still closed, but she could picture

Bhutano checking his watch before heading out of the room. Hearing the door close confirmed that he had left.

This wasn't good. They were getting ready to destroy the prison camps. It was genocide, and they were going to blame the extremists for the terrorist attack.

She had to alert Darshana. She cleared her mind and attempted to reach out to her. She knew Penny might see, but if she could get a message to Darshana and the elites could somehow intervene and obstruct the enemy's grand scheme, it would be worth it.

Darshana, please hear me.

The sound of a chair scraping against the floor caused Penny to open her eyes.

Naree stood before her, her nostrils flaring and her fists clenched at her sides. "You deceitful hag!"

A sudden pain in her hand exploded as her ring finger snapped. Avi stood behind Naree, black tendrils of smoke wafting from his hand. Penny cried out as the pain in her ring finger triggered the pain in her pinky finger. She felt as if half her hand had been run over by a tank.

Naree shook her head, teeth gritted together. "Will you never learn?"

Sweat drenched Penny's temples as she bared her teeth. "You are working with monsters! How could you sit idly by while Kashmeru destroys human life? Why would you let thousands of innocent people die?"

Rikuto curled his lips as she marched forward with the *tantō* knife. Penny gasped for breath. Before Rikuto could reach her, Kun put a hand up to stop him.

"Wait," Kun said, smirking. He cracked his knuckles and stretched out his neck. "I have a better idea."

Kun—the poisoner—extended his arms out toward her and twisted his wrists. Penny shuddered as acid filled her stomach. She felt as if her blood were curdling, and she doubled over in pain. It was as if she were being stabbed from the inside, her stomach being ripped to shreds. Bile rose in her throat as the acid threatened to bubble over and out of her. She fell onto all fours on the floor, heaving as her muscles felt like they were on fire.

"All right," Naree said. "That's enough."

Slowly, the stabbing pain stopped, but the acid was still lingering inside her.

"Though she doesn't deserve it, let's give her a moment to recover. She's proven to be a slow learner, but

I'm sure she'll cooperate from now on."

❧

Salina pulled Loni back behind a parked truck to duck out of sight as an Imperial Police car drove by. They were both quiet and standing still until the car was out of sight. As soon as it was gone, Loni yanked herself from Salina's grip and stomped off down the sidewalk.

"Hey," Salina called. "How about a *thank you*?"

Loni stopped and turned around. "Excuse me if I don't like being grabbed. Or do you not remember the last time you did that? I can show you a scar if you need a reminder."

Salina let out a slow breath, regretting that she had accidentally burned Loni back when they'd been in the academy. "Loni, I told you I didn't mean that. Tension was high. We were all hostile toward each other back then."

"But I never physically hurt *you*."

"I... I know."

Loni crossed her arms, waiting for her to continue.

Salina let out a grunt of frustration. "You know, why did you even volunteer to come with me if you can't stand being around me?"

"Let me be clear." Loni pointed a finger at her. "I didn't do this for you. I did this for Penny. At least *she* knows how to treat people. *She* knows what it's like to be a true friend."

They had been walking for what seemed like forever, trying to track down Penny's location, but every building, every house, had been a dead end. Darshana had linqed them to let them know Karina needed more time. They still hadn't covered the whole town yet, so Salina wasn't about to give up hope. But spending this much time with Loni alone was proving to be a tricky dance of not letting their past get in the way of their mission and focusing on what needed to be done before time ran out.

"Loni." Salina came closer to her, wanting to put a comforting hand on her shoulder but refraining. "I wish I could take it back. I'm sorry things became so unpleasant between us."

Loni pursed her lips. "I thought we were friends. The

four of us. And then when Huo-jin and Kanya broke up, it was as if I didn't matter to you anymore. Like we were suddenly enemies on opposite sides."

"We're not the same people we were back then, Loni. We've both been through a lot since then, and we've grown as people. And we know, now, what it's like to suffer loss. You're not the only one who's had to let go of someone who meant the world to them."

"Believe me, I know."

Salina dipped her head, knowing Loni was speaking about her sister who'd died in the government's attack on the academy. "We've both lost a lot."

Loni sighed. She studied Salina's face for a moment, as if she was searching for the right thing to say. "It might take some time to get over it. But I'll try."

It was quiet for a moment as they regarded each other. Salina wondered if they were finally at a point where they could bury the hatchet and move forward.

The chirping of her Linq stirred her from her thoughts. She checked the screen.

"It's Darshana." Salina scanned the area around her before she turned on her speakerphone. "Hey, Darshana, have you found the location?"

"We have the map, and Karina's done the spell. But it isn't narrowing it down enough. They must have some kind of magic blocking their exact location."

"How far has it narrowed down?" Salina asked. "Anything's better than nothing."

"I'll send you a picture of the area," Darshana told them. "Karina said she'll keep trying, but until she can get a precise location, you'll have to search on your own."

A chirp sounded. Salina held her Linq at arm's length so she and Loni could study the picture. It was zeroed in on a neighborhood. Salina checked the street names to try to figure out where they needed to go.

"Okay, got it," Salina said. She exchanged a look with Loni and gave her a nod. "We're headed there now."

"Good luck."

Fourteen

The copper glow in Shiro's palm fluttered and went out. Water pooled at his fingertips. He was trying to make an ice pick to try to free himself and Yuki from Kyoko's crimson foot trap, but his powers didn't seem to be working right. He blinked in confusion and shook out his hand.

"What's wrong?" Yuki asked.

"I don't know. I tried to push out my powers and they

fizzled."

"You think it's the comet?"

Shiro forced himself not to panic. "Could be. I'll try again."

This time, the glow held. In a matter of seconds, a shiny, solid ice pick formed in his hand. He breathed a sigh of relief and exchanged a look with Yuki.

Before he could even use the pick, the door to the small room opened. Rajim charged in, eyes wide, and placed his golden, glowing hands on the ice pick. It melted as Rajim pried it out of Shiro's hands.

"I guess I should have bound your hands as well," Kyoko said.

"Come on." Shiro swallowed hard. "You can't blame me for trying. You never said when you'd be back."

"I don't think you're in any position to make demands or excuses." Kyoko glanced over her shoulder. "Or did you not notice the roomful of mages we have on *our* side?"

Just then, a figure in the room caught Shiro's eye.

"Mitty!"

Both Kyoko and Rajim looked over their shoulders. In the room, Mitty—one of the mages who'd escaped with him and Qiang—squinted at Shiro.

"Oh, hey, Shiro," Mitty said. "What are you doing in there?"

Mitty, who was even bigger than Rajim, stomped closer. His hair was pulled back in a bun, and he was missing a tooth. Shiro suspected the tooth had been lost during their escape. Though, with the number of attacks the extremist group had been involved in, it could have been lost at any point in time.

"You know this guy?" Kyoko asked Mitty.

"Yeah. We were in the camps together. Got out together too. Well… sort of." Mitty shook his head at Shiro. "Where'd you go, man? We lost you back there."

"I got shot," Shiro explained. "Fell in the river."

"No way! And you survived?" Mitty whistled. "Dude, you must have nine lives."

"Maybe. Hey, Mitty, can you tell these two I know Qiang? We came here to talk to him."

Mitty approached Kyoko, raising a brow. "Enjoying your power trip, Kyoko?"

"Hey, I don't know these guys." Kyoko glared at Shiro. "They could be undercover."

"You can see they're mages."

"They could be double agents sent here by the government to usurp us."

Mitty scoffed. "I know paranoia drives you, but trust me. They're on our side."

Kyoko pursed her lips and held a hand out at Shiro's and Yuki's feet. The crimson stone disintegrated to powder. Her glare was still intense as Shiro and Yuki stood.

"Thank you," Shiro said. "Is Qiang here?"

Mitty waved for him to follow. "I'll take you to him."

As they walked through the auditorium, Mitty cast a look over his shoulder at Yuki. Shiro realized he didn't know who she was.

"This is Yuki, by the way."

Mitty smiled at her. "Nice to meet you, Yuki. What class of mage are you?"

"Diamond," she answered.

Mitty's eyes widened. "Really? I don't think I've met too many diamonds. They're rare."

"Yeah." Yuki cleared her throat. "I hear that a lot."

"I don't think we even have a diamond mage in the

rebellion." Mitty rubbed at his chin. "If you're thinking of joining, I could put in a good word for you."

Shiro flashed him a look. "Don't get any funny ideas, Mitty."

Yuki let out a small laugh. "It's okay, Shiro. He's just being nice. Trust me; I can tell."

Shiro gave her a nod. "If you say so."

"It's this way," Mitty said to them both as he gestured toward a staircase.

As they climbed the stairs, Shiro glanced at the crowd of mages who made up the extremist group. They were all following Qiang, all devoted to his purpose. He marveled at what Qiang had created, even if he didn't agree with his tactics.

When they reached the top of the stairs, Mitty opened the door to an office. Sitting in a chair by an electronic whiteboard was Peng, one of the two emerald mages who'd escaped the prison camps with him. The other emerald mage, Bao, was sitting at a desk typing on a computer. The two thin, long-legged men were not brothers, but—aside from Peng's red hair and hooked nose—they looked identical.

Leaning against the back wall, Qiang first narrowed his eyes, and then widened them, his thick brows raising in surprise. It might have simply been because Shiro hadn't seen him in a while, but Qiang appeared more handsome than ever, his body tall and lean, his shirt sleeves hugging the muscles in his arms, and there seemed to be a glow about his high cheekbones.

Qiang shook the hair out of his eyes. "Shiro?"

Shiro's heart pounded. The sound of Qiang's voice sent goosebumps over his skin, and Shiro's breath was caught in his throat.

"Man, Shiro," Peng said. "I knew you weren't dead."

Bao stood from the computer and walked over to pat Shiro on the arm. He then sidled up to Peng and pulled his Linq out. Peng did the same, and there was a beep when the two Linqs' heads touched. Shiro was about to accuse them of placing bets on his life, but he refrained. He was there to see Qiang.

Qiang took a few steps forward before his eyes went to Yuki. "Who have you brought me, Shiro?"

"This is Yuki. She's the diamond elite."

"Is that so?" Qiang asked. "Seems pretty young to be

both a diamond mage *and* an elite."

"Definitely pretty, though," Mitty added.

Out of the corner of his eye, Shiro spotted the white glow in Yuki's palms. The next second, Qiang, Peng, and Bao burst into giddy laughter. Peng bent over, holding his stomach. Bao wiped tears of laughter from his eyes. And Qiang—well, Shiro had never seen him laugh like that before. It made him smile. Mitty scratched his head, totally perplexed at what he was witnessing.

Yuki dropped her hands, and the white glow faded away. The three men sobered, clearing their throats as the laughing stopped.

Qiang blinked, running a hand over the stubble at his chin. "Okay. She's the diamond elite. Not sure making people laugh counts as a weapon, though."

"I needed to do something harmless," Yuki explained. "Instead of, oh, I don't know, something like this."

She raised her hand so fast, Shiro almost didn't catch the movement. Diamond bullets flew through the air with a zipping sound. Qiang stared in shock as the wall behind him was marked with gouges from where they'd made impact.

"*Damn*, girl," Mitty mumbled.

"If you can pry those out," Yuki said, "you can consider them my contribution to your cause."

Qiang gave her a sideways smirk, shaking his finger at her. "I like this one, Shiro."

Shiro gave him a nod. "With all due respect, that's not the reason I'm here."

"Okay." Qiang came nearer, closing the distance between them, sending a warm shiver up and down Shiro's spine. "What is it?"

"We overheard something at the governor's mansion," Shiro began.

"What were you doing there?" Qiang asked.

"He wasn't." Yuki raised her hand for a second. "I was. With a couple of other elites. We were in disguise—on a mission—when we overheard the chief of police and the director of the national census discussing something."

Shiro noticed she didn't mention the daggers and thought it was best if he didn't, either.

Qiang looked between them. "What were they discussing?"

Yuki let out a sigh. "They said they were going to

destroy the prison camps and blame it on the extremists. You."

Qiang studied her face. His gaze then went to Shiro. "I haven't heard this from any of my sources. But I'll look into it and find out what I can."

"Thank you, Qiang." Shiro gave him a slight bow.

"I'll deal with it because it's the right thing to do. But, Shiro, you might not agree on how I intend to stop them."

"I wish it wouldn't come down to violence." Shiro gave a small nod. "But I also understand you'll do what you have to do to save our people."

There was a small hint of a smile on Qiang's face. He took Shiro's hands, rubbing his thumbs against his knuckles. Shiro let out a shuddered breath, a fluttery feeling filling his stomach.

"Can Shiro and I have a moment alone?" Qiang asked the room.

Yuki gave Shiro a questioning look, to which Shiro responded with a nod to let her know it was all right.

Everyone cleared out and left them alone to speak privately. The moment the door closed behind them, Qiang pulled Shiro into his arms.

"I want you to know, I mourned you. I thought you were dead."

Shiro buried his head in Qiang's shoulder, breathing in the scent of sandalwood and musk. "I thought you gave up on me."

"I wouldn't have, had I known you survived." Qiang stepped back and locked gazes with Shiro. "I promise, when this is all over and both of us manage to stay alive, I'll find you."

Qiang placed a slow kiss upon Shiro's lips. Shiro felt lightheaded, fully aware of the beating of his heart. When the kiss ended, they embraced once more, and Qiang caressed the back of Shiro's head.

Though Shiro wanted the embrace to last forever, he knew he couldn't stay. They exchanged Linq numbers to keep in touch and update each other on their progress, and in a blur of longing and heartbreak, they parted.

Shiro's mind replayed the kiss and Qiang's promise as he and Yuki left the theater. They'd done what they'd come to do, and they stepped into the night with a small sense of relief.

Halfway down the street, Yuki turned to him, placing

a hand on his back. "He truly cares about you, you know?"

He was about to question her but closed his mouth, knowing she had used her powers to read Qiang's emotions. Allowing himself a small moment to take in that fact, Shiro smiled.

Fifteen

Four hundred feet above the village of Bhaja, in the city of Pune, a group of twenty-two rock-cut caves comprised of prayer halls called *stupas* made up the famous Bhaja Caves. Jae stared up at the structure, feeling exhausted. His legs were weak, and his slack of sleep was causing waves of hot and cold to wash over him. He wasn't sure if the ringing in his ears was because of the messed-up magic from the approaching comet or because he and Mayhara had driven the entire night non-stop.

"I feel mentally numb," Mayhara said as she stretched out her back. "I was so afraid I'd fall asleep and fall off the bike."

Jae raked a hand through his hair. "Same here. I think we better eat something and hope the rise of insulin wakes us up."

Mayhara opened her backpack. "Protein bar?"

"And an energy drink, I think."

The smallest hint of a smile flashed across her face as she handed him the provisions.

"So, what's the plan?" she asked between bites.

Jae took out a pamphlet of the Caves. "I was looking at Karina's notes, and I think one of the translations she wrote down matches with cave number eight in the structure."

Mayhara looked at the graphic of the spot Jae pointed at. "Why do you think that?"

"Out of all the caves, it's the only one that is partially destroyed. One of Karina's translations was the word 'broken.' I think that fits."

"Only one way to find out." Mayhara chugged her

drink. "You ready?"

Jae pulled out his Linq. "One second. Apparently, Shiro sent me a text. He says there's a scroll hidden in the spine of the grimoire. An important one." Jae tucked the Linq away. "I guess we should make sure it's intact when we find it."

"Did he say what was important about it?"

"No. But we can sort all that out after we actually get our hands on it."

"True."

Tours of the Caves took place daily. Jae and Mayhara posed as tourists as they bought their tickets. Along with Mayhara's head scarf, she also wore a pair of sunglasses to hide her eyes. Jae, who still had the baseball cap he'd stolen from the festival, donned sunglasses as well.

The Caves were beautiful and rich with cultural and religious history, but Jae knew he had to concentrate on their mission. When they got to the eighth cave, Jae and Mayhara hung back from the crowds, pretending to inspect the sign that explained the history of the cave.

Jae ran his hands along the texture of the stone walls, waiting until there was a gap in the crowds of tourists.

When no one was around to witness, he put his hand on the small of Mayhara's back and led her through the entrance of the cave.

At first there wasn't much to see, short of some wooden beams and a section that looked like it had collapsed, but as they made their way to the rear wall of the cave, Jae noticed a symbol on the wall. It was almost invisible to the eye, but the bumps and grooves were definitely there.

"I need the scroll," he said, keeping his voice to a whisper.

"Did you find something?" Mayhara pulled out the scroll from the backpack, checking over her shoulder that no one else was coming into the cave.

"I think so."

Mayhara kept watch as Jae checked the scroll.

"It doesn't look like it lines up with any of the lines," Jae said. "Is this symbol in Karina's translations?"

"Let me check."

Jae ran his fingers over the symbol and inspected the cracks in the wall as Mayhara checked Karina's list.

"Pull," she said.

Jae wrinkled his brow. "You sure it's not 'push'?"

"It says 'pull.'"

Jae felt around for something to grasp on to—a lever or a latch or even a groove deep enough for his fingers—but found nothing. "I'm not sure how anyone is supposed to pull on this wall. There's nothing to pull."

Mayhara studied the wall for a moment. "Because it's not supposed to be pulled open by just anyone. It's supposed to be a witch. Pulling it open with magic."

Jae felt his throat close up and his hope fizzle. When he mumbled a curse, Mayhara let out a small laugh.

"What so funny?" Jae asked.

"Oh, I don't know. Can you think of another way we can move a big hunk of rock?"

She raised a brow, and Jae had to smirk.

He playfully bowed and held his hand out toward the wall. "Of course. Be my guest."

Jae stepped back as Mayhara raised her hands, palms aimed at the wall and glowing red. The floor shook as the wall began to rumble. Sand and debris fell as the part of the wall Mayhara used her powers on pivoted like a big, thick door. Beyond it was an abyss of darkness and the stale scent of dust.

When the opening was wide enough for them to fit through, Mayhara lowered her hands. Jae glanced at the entrance of the cave to make sure no one was watching.

Mayhara adjusted the strap of her backpack. "Ladies first?"

"Only if you're sure."

"I can use my powers to feel the ground and walls and make sure we're not suddenly stepping into a pitfall."

"Good idea." He threw a look over his shoulder one last time. "And we better hurry and close this behind us before someone notices. Or follows us in."

They slipped inside, and Jae used his Linq light to illuminate the area they'd stepped into. The red glow of Mayhara's crimson power shone as she closed the secret door. The scraping sound of rock and sand echoed in the chamber as the external light was shut out.

Mayhara's palms glowed as she held her hands out in front of her. "Okay, this way."

It was difficult to see because Jae's Linq light was bright against the old, dusty walls, but he could discern that they were in a narrow passageway riddled with spiderwebs and moss that had grown between stones. Mayhara was quiet as she led them down the passageway, the sound of her breathing steady. After a minute, the narrow corridor opened up to a larger, circular cavern. In the middle of the cavern was a pile of rocks covered with a large slab of stone.

Mayhara put her hands on the slab. "There's something under here. A large space."

"You think it's a trapdoor or something?"

"I'm not sure. But I can move this off so we can see."

Jae stepped back as Mayhara used her powers to move the stone slab. It noisily scraped against the pile of rocks until it cleared them. Once it was removed, they could see that it wasn't just a pile of rocks, but a circular structure resembling a well.

They moved forward and tried to look into the well, Jae's light shining on a deep shaft surrounded by slick, brick-like stones. His light would only travel so far.

"I hear water," he said. "A waterfall, I think."

"There are waterfalls at some of the Caves, right?"

"Yeah. Maybe this leads to one. Or is fed by one."

"I wonder how far down it goes." She created glowing

particles and dropped them into the well. The tiny lights traveled down so far that they were impossible to see, disappearing into the abyss.

"You think we need to go down there?" Jae asked.

She ran her hand along the top of the stones. "I think there's a symbol carved into these rocks. Let's check it against Karina's translations."

Jae pulled out the translations and compared the symbol to Karina's list. "Downward."

Mayhara sighed. "I guess we go down. But maybe I can make it a little easier for us. Can you light it up again?"

Jae held his Linq in the well, lighting up the rocks. Mayhara lowered her hand into the well, the glow of red filling the shaft. One by one, stones began to protrude from the well wall, every foot or so, forming footholds and handholds.

Jae smirked. "That'll make it a lot easier."

"It's still slippery, so move with caution." Mayhara waited as Jae packed away Karina's translations. "You ready?"

"Yeah." He let out a hard breath. "Let's go."

Mayhara sat on the edge of the well wall and swung

her legs over into the hole. As she found her footing, Jae readied himself, tucking away his Linq.

Jae, please.

He hesitated, getting a chill from his sister's voice in his head. Especially now, in the dark.

Jae, you must help me. Kashmeru demands the daggers. If I don't hand them over to the Pishacha, he'll have me killed.

Though Jae's instinct was to listen to his sister's pleas, he tried to ignore her, knowing it was a trick. He forced himself to take steady breaths as he sat on the edge of the well wall, ready to follow Mayhara down.

They'll kill me, Jae. Do you want that to happen?

He felt a cinch in his heart. "Of course I don't."

"What?" Mayhara called from inside the well.

"N-Nothing." He shook his head, even though Mayhara couldn't see him from where she was. "It's Naree again."

"She's trying to distract you. Come on."

He knew she was right. Kashmeru was using her to manipulate the elites. Jae squared his jaw, forcing himself to concentrate on the task at hand, and lowered himself into the well.

The climb down was slippery and grueling. It seemed to take forever, foothold after foothold, with only their glowing palms reflecting against the stones lighting the way. At long last, he heard Mayhara grunt along with the sound of a splash.

"I've reached the bottom," she called up at him. "I'm ankle-deep in water."

Jae looked down as he descended the final few feet. He could see the light from Mayhara's Linq illuminating the water below. He jumped when the walls of the well came to an end and landed in a small stream of water that swallowed his feet.

Mayhara already had the scroll out and was checking the map as she glanced around. "There's a tunnel here. I think this is where the map on the scroll begins."

After about twenty feet, they came to a fork in the path.

"This way," Mayhara said after studying the map.

Another twenty feet, and the ground rose above the water. The tunnel curved to the right, getting tighter. Jae wondered if they had picked the right way, but Mayhara was following the map on the scroll, so he gave her the benefit of the doubt. When the tunnel widened again, he was glad he hadn't questioned her.

After they walked a bit more, they came to a section where the tunnel forked off in multiple directions. Mayhara stopped, tilting her head as she brought the map closer to her face.

"What is it?" Jae asked.

"This section isn't shown on the map."

He came closer to take a look for himself. Their heads were right next to each other, and he could hear her breaths. The faint smell of vanilla and jasmine wafted around him. He had to force himself to not think about how close she was to him, but instead to figure out their path.

"What about this symbol here?" he asked, pointing to a mark on the map that stood alone along a line.

"There are no forks in the road there, but maybe that's part of the puzzle." She lifted her head, glancing around. "Look to see if this symbol is marked on any of the tunnel entrances."

Using their Linq lights, they searched the walls of the tunnels, feeling for carvings or grooves and bumps. Jae hadn't found anything yet, and he tried desperately to fight off the feeling of defeat.

"Wait," Mayhara called.

Jae felt a weight lift off his heart. He hurried to her side, to where she was crouching on the ground. Her fingers ran over some cracks in the floor of the tunnel.

She checked the symbol on the map once more. "This is it."

It was barely recognizable, but she was right. They stood and continued down the tunnel.

"It's like a maze," Mayhara said.

"More like a labyrinth."

"What's the difference?"

"There's only one way out of a labyrinth. It's a good thing we have this map. Witches can be very clever in hiding things. And with something as important as the grimoire at stake, I'm willing to bet the other corridors don't lead to just dead ends. There could be traps that could kill someone."

Mayhara shuddered, shaking out her shoulders.

"Who do you think carved out these tunnels?" Jae asked.

"It's a hefty job. I'm guessing the witches were working with some crimson mages. I can imagine a team of them would be able to carry out the construction of these tunnels.

After another hundred feet or so, the tunnel opened up to a large cavern. Jae's eyes widened as he took in the sight before them. It was like a giant, underground storage room. The space was filled with a cornucopia of items. Jae figured some, if not all of them, were magical. Old, withered books were piled on what looked like an altar. There was a pile of materials, and when Jae got closer to inspect, he lifted one to find it was a cloak of some kind. A silver telescope stood amongst a stack of other objects he couldn't begin to identify. There were shelves of jars containing various liquids and items. A chill ran up and down his spine at the thought of what vile things might be inside.

"What is all this stuff?" Mayhara's voice was a whisper, as if she were afraid to wake something that might be sleeping in the cavern.

"I don't know, exactly." He picked up a gold hourglass to inspect it. A glittery liquid swirled inside. "But I'm willing to bet some of it's worth a fortune."

Mayhara nodded. "Hidden here by the witches. Probably for good reason. We just need to find where the grimoire is hidden." She checked the map. "There are a series of symbols here. Four of them in a row. Maybe the grimoire is labeled with them?"

He took a look at the symbols. "Maybe. Let's start looking."

They began searching through the things, going first through the pile of books. Something standing beneath a stack of canisters caught Jae's eye. At first, he thought it was a low table, but when he crouched down to inspect it, he realized it was a chest.

He removed the items that were stacked on top of the chest and ran a hand along the surface. It was made of a dark wood and adorned with intricate carvings. When his eyes went along the edge of the lid, he spotted a number of symbols that were similar to the ones on the map.

"Mayhara, take a look at this."

"What did you find?"

"The symbols on the edge of this lid. Some of them look like they match the ones on the map."

She crouched down next to him and ran her fingers along the symbols. "Yeah, you're right. But there are a lot more than the four in the scroll. There must be twenty different symbols here."

Jae placed his hands on the lid and tried to pry the chest open. It wouldn't budge. Mayhara joined him as he tried again.

"Let me try my powers," she said when it didn't work.

Her palms lit up in glowing red, her gaze intense as she pushed out her powers. But still, the lid wouldn't budge.

"Sealed with magic," Jae mumbled.

"Then why the symbols on the map?" She looked at the map again, her eyes flitting to the lid every few seconds. "Wait. It's a combination."

Hope sprung in Jae's heart. He watched with a quiver in his stomach as Mayhara pressed the symbol on the chest's lid that matched the first symbol on the scroll. The wood shifted inward, as if it were a button she had pressed. Her eyes widened, the small hint of a smile on her lips. She searched for the second symbol and pressed it, then the third and fourth.

The popping sound of a metal latch opening filled the cavern. Jae and Mayhara glanced at each other with anticipation and then inched forward, placing their hands on the lid. Together, they pried the lid of the chest open. There was a thunderous *crash* as it hit the back wall, exposing the open chest.

Mayhara swallowed visibly. Jae held his breath as Mayhara reached in and pulled out a dusty book. She and Jae exchanged a look, and Jae was almost frightened to believe their luck.

They'd found the grimoire.

Sixteen

Penny felt as if her mind were being pulled in a million different directions. She had a clear picture of the daggers in her mind, but her visions were jumbled, scattered, and blending into each other.

"Are you sure she's the elite?" It was Ru who'd spoken.

Penny opened her eyes to see her carving into the table with the *tantō*.

"I think she's bluffing," Jin-woo said.

Penny squared her jaw. "The daggers are not easy to find. If they were, anyone would be able to find them."

Naree held a hand up, gesturing for everyone to stop quarreling. "No one asked for commentary. Penny just needs to get out of her own way and concentrate harder."

Penny jumped when the door opened. Bhutano entered the room, and Penny's mind brought up the words he had spoken before. He'd said he was meeting with the governor to discuss the prison camps. A sick twisting wormed its way through Penny's stomach as she considered what they might have decided to do. She felt helpless to stop the enemy from carrying out their plan. She hoped that Jae had remembered Bhutano's conversation at the ball and somehow devised a plan to thwart their efforts. Only time would tell.

"Tell me," Bhutano said, "have we found out the location of the daggers yet?"

"Not yet," Naree answered.

He straightened the lapels of his uniform jacket. "Kashmeru is growing impatient. The comet gets closer every minute and we don't have the daggers *or* the grimoire."

"We'll get the information out of her," Naree insisted.

"Well, perhaps we're thinking too small. No more messing with little fingers. I think we should aim for something bigger. Like her legs."

Penny held back a gasp. Her hand was in enough pain as it was. She couldn't fathom what it would be like to have her legs crushed to the point of not being able to walk anymore. And Avi wouldn't hesitate to do it, either. They didn't need her to walk. They only needed her to talk. Penny bit the inside of her cheek, knowing she had to oblige.

"I'll do it," she said. "I'll find them."

Naree shifted in her chair, smiling. "That's more like it."

"No more games, amethyst mage." Bhutano crossed his arms over his chest. "You best deliver or be ready to deal with my wrath."

Penny swallowed hard and nodded. Closing her eyes, she pushed all thoughts from her mind. This time, she forced herself to really concentrate on the daggers, to bring to mind what they looked like and what they felt like. She remembered holding one in her hand and inspecting it.

The shiny blade, the intricate design of the hilt, the elegant box it was stored in.

The image of a dagger solidified in her mind, but as she zoomed out, the location was unclear.

"Do you see them?" Bhutano's voice was harsh and impatient.

"No." Penny kept her eyes closed as she shook her head. "Not them. Just one."

"What do you mean?" he asked.

She furrowed her brow. "I don't see the others. I… I don't think the daggers are together."

Hearing a loud crash and Bhutano's roar of anger, Penny jumped in her seat, but she kept her eyes closed so as not to further infuriate the man.

She felt soft hands on her arms and felt Naree come even further into her mind.

"She's right," Naree said. "It's just one dagger. Buried, near a stream. But it's unclear. I don't recognize the area."

"Search harder," Bhutano ordered. "Kashmeru demands it."

Penny pushed her powers out and reached for one of the mages. If she could see one of them, maybe she would have a better idea of what had happened to the daggers. Flashes of light and fragments of images passed through her mind in a dizzying display until finally, it landed on Jae.

Penny believed it was Naree's connection to him that made him pop into her mind so easily.

She zoomed out her focus on him and found him in a strange cave, crouching beside Mayhara. Mayhara ran her hand over the leather cover of an old book covered with dust.

Naree gasped. "What's this?"

Penny realized what they were looking at. They'd found the grimoire that contained the spell that would unlock Kashmeru from his tomb. But now Naree saw it as well. Penny scrambled to clear her mind. "Nothing. I don't know what that was."

"Liar."

The harshness of Naree's voice made Penny's eyes shoot open.

Naree whipped her head around to face Bhutano. "It's the grimoire. They now have it."

Bhutano lifted his chin, the corner of his mouth

inching upward. "Very good, young mage. You've unwittingly disclosed the last piece of the puzzle we need to complete Kashmeru's awakening and saved us the trouble of fetching it."

Penny bit back a curse. Now Jae and Mayhara would be even bigger targets than they had been before. There was nothing she could do to stop the Pishacha from going after the grimoire, and it was just a matter of time before they found out where all the daggers were hidden.

"We have had a witch trying to track down that old book, since we couldn't get the information from the swamp witch." Bhutano checked his watch. "But now that it is within our reach, we can have the witch concentrate on learning the spell to break the bond that locks Kashmeru's tomb."

"And then I can be reunited with my true love," Naree added, her eyes softening.

"Do you have the location?" Bhutano asked.

Penny tensed all her muscles, trying to block the information from Naree's sight. But it was a futile attempt.

"I know where it is. Yes." Naree stood from the chair

and faced Bhutano. "The Bhaja Caves. They're underground. In some secret tunnel."

Bhutano snapped his fingers. "Ru. Jin-woo. Get to the Caves and do whatever you deem necessary to retrieve the grimoire."

Penny swallowed hard as the two dark mages disappeared, leaving clouds of black smoke behind them.

Salina and Loni approached the massive iron gate of an exquisite villa. Behind the gate, the front lawn sported a lush garden of manicured bushes and thick, green grass. The stone pathway that led up to the house was impeccably clean, flanked by purple Aubrieta flowers on either side. On the wide stone porch, an Imperial Police officer stood guard.

Salina narrowed her eyes as a man dressed in black with a mouth mask came out of the house and spoke to the guard. The guard nodded and went around the back of the house, and the masked man went back inside.

"Was that a Pishacha soldier speaking to the officer?" Loni asked.

"Yeah," Salina answered. "I guess we got the right house."

"Did you see that?" Loni pointed to the front door.

"No. What?"

"He didn't put a code in the lock pad. I think it's unlocked."

Salina put her hands on the bars of the gate. "But this gate isn't. Tell me if you see someone coming."

Loni scanned the area as Salina put her hand on the gate's lock pad. The golden glow of her palm lit up the device until it emitted a low beep, and the red light on the device went out.

"What did you do?" Loni asked.

"I overheated the circuits. It crashed the system, but we need to hurry before it restarts."

They pushed the gate open and slipped through, closing the gate before the lock pad rebooted. Using the landscape to help them approach, Salina and Loni managed to get to the front door undetected.

Salina wasn't sure where the officer had gone, but she

didn't want to stick around to find out. Luckily, the entry to the house was laden with windows. She peeked inside to make sure the coast was clear and then pushed on the latch of the door. It opened without incident.

"You were right," Salina whispered. "Let's go."

The interior of the house was like nothing Salina had ever seen. The temple had been gorgeous, but this villa had a unique modern look to it.

Telling herself she needed to focus on the task at hand instead of the villa's decorative style, Salina scanned the area and listened for movement.

As the two of them got to the main room, a figure moved at their side.

Pishacha.

Salina clenched her jaw and pulled up her golden powers. At her side, Loni did the same with her emerald powers. Together, they launched a torrential gust of fire at the Pishacha, who flailed as his cloak caught the flames. Just as Salina and Loni were about to throw another offensive strike, the Pishacha disappeared.

The sound of fast footfalls echoed down a side hall.

"This way," Salina exclaimed.

She and Loni took off down the corridor. They made it to the end in time to see a dark mage about to descend a staircase.

The dark mage shot black particles at them before darting down the stairs. Loni held up her hands, and a glowing wave of green knocked the particles to the wayside before the black light could make impact with them. The two of them took off after the dark mage and found a door at the bottom of the stairs.

The dark mage had had no time to stop their advancement, and Loni and Salina crashed into the basement room. There, sitting in a chair, her legs bound with what looked like vines, was Penny.

"Loni! Salina!" Penny tried to stand, but her bound legs made it difficult.

Taking a defensive stance were three dark mages, two Pishacha, the chief of police, and Naree.

Though they were outnumbered, Salina figured they had the element of surprise on their side.

Salina thrust out her hands, and golden fire raced out at two of the Pishacha, knocking them back. A rush of wind was sent out by Loni, which raced over the floor and knocked one of the dark mage's legs out from under him.

Another dark mage lifted his hands, black tendrils of smoke swirling through the air at Salina. She summoned a fire whip and slashed it through the air, whipping his energy away. She snapped it once more, and the whip caught around his waist. He cried out in pain as the fire burned him. Salina cracked the whip to the side and sent the dark mage crashing into the wall. One of the Pishacha grabbed him and they disappeared together.

Penny lifted her hands, the purple glow set in her palms. The room began to cloud up in purple smog, but suddenly, she dropped her hands and cried out in pain. Salina's jaw dropped, and she had to blink, unsure of what had happened.

The chief of police—or Bhutano, as they had learned he truly was—advanced on Salina. A sneer grew on his face, and he pulled out his taser-pistol from his holster. Behind him, Naree grabbed Penny and held her by the neck.

Salina raised her hands toward Bhutano, who was fast upon her. She aimed her fire whip, but before she could strike, a blade flew through the air and hit him, slicing into his heart. Salina gasped. She looked over to see that it had been Loni who'd used her air powers to send the knife—a *tantō*—at him. He stopped in his tracks, staring down at his chest, which was gushing blood.

"No," Naree called out, her brows drawn together. Her grip tightened on Penny.

Bhutano stumbled backward but kept on his feet. He quickly turned toward Naree and teetered to her, grabbing on to Penny's arms and staring into her face.

Salina readied herself, unsure of what Bhutano was going to do.

With his hands clamped on to Penny, he muttered something Salina couldn't hear. Naree's eyes widened. Dark dust and smoke surround all three of them before the police chief crumpled to the ground. Penny's head fell back, and her eyes fluttered shut.

The remaining Pishacha and the two dark mages hurried to Naree, who was propping up the now-unconscious Penny. Sneers covered their faces as the black cloaks of the Pishacha wrapped around them all, and in an instant, they disappeared in a swirling cloud of black smoke, leaving Loni and Salina gaping in shock. Left behind, the police chief lay dead on the ground, his blank eyes staring up at them.

Seventeen

Darshana wiped the sweat from Amalia's brow as Amalia recited the last lines of the power transfer incantation to Karina. She tried not to wince at the raspy sound of Amalia's breathing, choosing instead to concentrate on the dampness of the cotton cloth. Karina carefully wrote down the lines, repeating them back to her grandmother to make sure she'd gotten them right. They'd been sitting with Amalia for over an hour, making sure they got all the information about the ritual written down, as she insisted.

"Are you sure you got it, dear?" Amalia's voice was hoarse and gruff.

"Yes," Karina answered. "I checked every word."

"You were always a clever young woman." Amalia gave her a small nod. "Best student I ever had."

Karina's mouth turned into a slight smirk. "I thought I was your only student."

Amalia took her hand. "It was my greatest achievement, teaching you. I know you'll be able to do this. I totally believe in you."

The last word was cut off by dry coughs followed by wheezes. Amalia pressed a hand to her chest, her face twisted in pain.

"Grandmother?" Karina stood, setting the notebook and pen down on the nightstand.

Darshana reached for Amalia's shoulders, trying to help her sit up. Karina grabbed a glass of water and tried to offer it to her, but Amalia waved her off, shaking her head. Amalia cleared her throat, her eyes watering. When Karina set the glass of water down, Amalia took her hand.

"Karina, you have… an important role… in all of this. Don't… forget. Make me proud… and save the world."

Karina nodded as she bit her lip. "I will, Grandmother."

Amalia slowly turned her head to Darshana. "Take care… of her, Darshana.

Darshana set a gentle hand on her arm. "I promise. I will."

Amalia nodded slowly and turned to Karina again. Her hand trembled as she raised it to stroke Karina's cheek. "I… love you… Karina." Her last word came out as air.

Karina's tears were flowing, and Amalia's eyes fluttered closed. Her ragged breathing slowed, and then her mouth dropped open as the last breath left her body.

Darshana wiped the flowing tears from her cheeks. It felt as if her heart were folding in on itself, each beat sending a heavy, biting ache through her body. She could only imagine what Karina was going through, losing the woman who was practically her mother, the woman who'd raised her and taught her everything she knew, cared for her from when she'd been an infant until she'd blossomed into a young woman. The woman who had been her everything.

Karina dropped her head to her grandmother's arm, her hold still tight on her hand. Her body shook as she sobbed uncontrollably.

Even if she weren't an empath, it would have been unbearable. But as it was, Darshana had to leave the room. She thought it was respectful, in any case, to give Karina time and space to mourn.

As she closed the door and stood in the hall, she felt lightheaded and had to balance herself by holding the wall. Her sobs shook her, and she let them come. She, too, needed to mourn.

A noise from the main room snapped her from her grief, and she forced herself to regain her composure. When she reached the main room and spotted Shiro and Yuki, she almost burst into tears again. Their sad faces reflected her own.

"I have some bad news," she said to them.

Yuki nodded, wringing her hands. "We know. Amalia is no longer with us. I felt it."

Darshana stepped forward, and Yuki and Shiro closed

the distance to embrace her as she cried.

"We were friends for a long time," Darshana said as the tears dissipated. She took a step back and wiped her cheeks. "We studied together when we were young. But even as life took us in separate directions, we remained friends. We only saw each other once a year, perhaps, but we always picked up where we'd left off. No matter the time in between."

Yuki squeezed her hand. "I'm sorry for your loss."

"I'm sorry I couldn't help her." Shiro shook his head.

Darshana patted his arm. "Do not blame yourself. This was not your fault, but the fault of the enemy. They did this to her, and we must not let her death be in vain."

Yuki nodded, her gaze trained on the floor.

The sound of Shiro's Linq chirping disrupted the moment.

Shiro checked the screen. "It's Salina."

Darshana nodded, and Shiro pressed the button for the speakerphone.

"Salina," he said, "did you find Penny?"

"We… did." Salina sounded hesitant. "But there was trouble. A battle. Loni killed Bhutano."

Shiro's eyes widened. The three of them exchanged looks.

"Do you have Penny?" Yuki asked.

There was a pause.

"No," Salina said. "They took her and disappeared. Penny is gone."

Eighteen

They were almost out of the well. Jae climbed after Mayhara, forcing himself not to curse every time his foot slipped on the footholds. He wasn't going to let the difficult climb get him down. They'd found the grimoire. They had all the daggers. Things were looking up for them.

Mayhara let out a grunt as she reached the top of the well. Jae could just make out the glow of her palms as she grasped on to the edge to lift herself up.

Just then, a low howl sounded in the well. Jae glanced down to see black smoke swirling below him.

Jae whipped his head back toward Mayhara. "Hurry! Get out of the well."

Mayhara gasped, looking down to see what Jae saw.

The Pishacha were there.

Black tendrils of dark magic swirled around him like a rope, tightening around his body. A look down revealed a dark mage sneering at him, directly below his feet. A hand clamped around Jae's foot. He kicked, nearly losing his hold on the brick Mayhara had turned into a handhold.

Above him, Mayhara stood above the well, having cleared herself from it. She had her hands extended, and red crimson energy shot downward. Jae's foot was released, and he looked down to see the dark mages and Pishacha slipping rapidly down the well shaft. Mayhara had gotten rid of the other footholds, giving them nothing to hold on to.

"Hurry!" she called out, extending a hand to him.

Jae forced his legs to go faster. Below him, clouds of black smoke revealed that the Pishacha had disappeared with the dark mages.

Mayhara yanked on Jae's arm and pulled him out of the well. She was just lifting the stone slab of the well, intending on sealing it, when she was hit with a downpour of rocks from behind. The rocks pushed her to the ground, and Jae had to hurry to pull her free from the weight of them.

In the cavern, opposite them, stood two dark mages and two Pishacha. One of the dark mages Jae recognized as Ru, the daughter of Director Shei. She was the one who had attacked Mayhara with the rocks. The other dark mage was the one who'd tried to pull Jae down in the well. He had short hair and dark skin, with shaved lines cut into his brows. Other than his menacing sneer, he had a mysteriously beautiful face.

Jae and Mayhara moved away from the well and adopted defensive stances, their hands raised, palms facing their enemies.

The dark-skinned mage aimed his hands outward. Black tendrils swirled around the cavern, some of them sinking into the well. In the next instant, massive, reaching vines slithered up and out of the well, along with a barrage of creeping insects, chirping and droning as they crawled out of the well and wriggled toward them. There were so many of them that Jae couldn't see the cavern floor anymore.

Mayhara shuddered and closed her eyes for a moment, most likely trying to block the image from her mind. She held up her hands, the blinding flash of red light pulsing in her palms as the earth moved. Gaps and holes were created, swallowing the insects into its depths bit by bit.

Jae's head snapped back as a sphere of black energy struck him in the head, sending him tumbling back. He retaliated by throwing both hands forward. Glowing particles of sapphire energy flared as he hurled them at the dark mage who'd attacked him. The dark mage grunted as he was knocked back and crashed against the stone wall.

Ru stomped one foot forward as she pushed out her powers, tossing a large boulder at Mayhara. With eyes wide in shock, Mayhara was quick to dive toward Jae, pushing him out of the way and getting them both a safe distance from the boulder. A massive crash sounded as the boulder hit the well, destroying both at impact.

As Jae lifted his head, he realized the contents of

Mayhara's backpack had spilled all over the cavern floor. He gasped as he spotted the grimoire lying a couple of feet away.

He reached for it, but he was lifted from the ground by black smoke and hurled across the room. His head slammed into the wall, causing everything to momentarily go black.

Mayhara scrambled to the grimoire and held it to her chest. She turned, held her palm up, and let her powers go. Crimson particles wrapped around her like a shield, blocking her from everyone's view.

Ru growled and her power pulsed in the air. The crimson shield cracked and then fractured, and a deafening eruption filled the room as the shield was obliviated, sending rock and sand and earth sailing in all directions. Jae just caught sight of Mayhara darting from the explosion before he was grabbed by one of the Pishacha and thrown toward the dark-skinned mage. Jae's body was flipped around by the dark mage, and in the next second, Jae was punched in the jaw. He mustered all his energy to retaliate, striking the dark mage in the stomach.

Blow for blow, the punches struck over and over, like

pounding drums in a volatile dance.

There was a roar in the cavern, and Jae turned in time to see a pulse of energy erupt from Ru's hands. Jae and the dark mage were thrown in opposite directions. When Jae turned his head, he spotted Ru's arm wrapped around Mayhara's neck as she ripped the book from her hands.

The dark-skinned mage smirked at Jae right before he was enveloped in the black cape of the Pishacha soldier at his side. Ru quickly backed up into the other Pishacha soldier, her glare still set on Mayhara. In an instant, they were gone, and black smoke filled the room.

Jae felt his stomach drop. He rushed to Mayhara, both of them coughing from the smoke.

Mayhara took his hand and led them to the room's secret door. A red glow appeared as the smoke began to dwindle, and the sound of the stone door scraping against sand and dirt reverberated in their ears.

They stumbled out into the cave, which was fortunately vacant. Mayhara doubled over, coughing. Jae put his hands on her arms and helped her to stand.

"Are you all right?" Jae pushed her hair back and checked her face.

She placed a hand on his arm, gasping for breath. "Yeah, I'm okay. What about you?"

"Just some cuts and bruises." He glanced back at the opening to the secret passage, spots flashing in his vision. "They got the grimoire."

She let out a breath. "I'm sorry. I couldn't stop them from taking it." She reached behind her and pulled something out from beneath her jacket. "But they didn't get this."

Jae's eyes widened as Mayhara held her hand up. His throat closed up as he gasped for breath, unable to believe what he was seeing. Clasped in the safety of her fingers was a tiny scroll.

"Is that—?"

"Yes. I took it out of the grimoire's spine without them seeing." She shook her head. "We're not lost yet."

The story continues in

Amethyst Mage

TURN THE PAGE
FOR A
PREVIEW OF
AMETHYST MAGE,
BOOK SIX
IN THE
EMPIRE OF THE LOTUS
SERIES

One

The breeze that blew over the meadow was unusually warm. It made Karina think of the swamp—their home—and she knew her grandmother would have been pleased.

Karina swept her dark hair out of her face as she continued to consecrate the meadow—a piece of land on Mr. Kitaro's property—with her mixture of sandalwood, patchouli, and jasmine oils. She repeated the blessing as she paced the ground surrounding her grandmother's grave. Once the blessing was complete, Jae and Shiro lowered the satin cocoon that was wrapped around Amalia's body, placing the deceased swamp witch in her grave.

Karina was the first to toss a handful of earth onto her grandmother's body. She did so with a tightened jaw and a heavy heart. Steadying her breaths, she forced herself not to break down. Not now. She had a ritual she needed to complete before she could allow herself to let the grief crawl in.

Darshana, the wise guru that led the mages, followed suit, gently throwing dirt upon the silk cocoon. She stood back, gazing upon the corpse of her lost friend, and closed her eyes as wind played with the hair of her long, white braid.

The others soon fell in line. Once they'd all had their turn, Jae and Shiro filled the grave. Watching her grandmother slowly disappearing beneath the soil, Karina took deep, heavy breaths and prepared herself for the incantation.

It was as if any sense of happiness or joy was being

buried along with her grandmother. Her heart felt like a stone in her chest. It was a struggle just to stand. But she'd made a promise, and she intended to keep it.

Once the grave was filled, Mr. Kitaro—the Sacred Key that had accompanied the mages for much of their journey—handed each of the elite mages a candle. The mages spread out, equidistant from each other, surrounding the grave. Darshana moved away to stand beside Mr. Kitaro, and Karina, with a trembling breath, gave them a nod.

Closing her eyes, Karina recited the words of the incantation her grandmother taught her. When she got through all the verses once, she opened her eyes and spread out her arms.

Each of the six mages held their candles secure in their left hands as they held out their right, palms facing Amalia's grave.

Karina began the incantation again. She would have to repeat it until the transfer of power was complete. Her grandmother's witch powers would first return to the earth, which was bonded with her magic. The incantation would pull those powers from the consecrated earth and guide them to Karina, who would then absorb her grandmother's magic and combine it with her own. The mages served as a power booster, the pull of their elements guiding as much magic as possible to its new home base.

Amalia had said even one mage involved in the spell would supply enough power to amplify the transfer. Penny—the elite amethyst mage—was still missing, but Karina's spell was still empowered immensely by the remaining six elites.

It was the red glow of Mayhara's power—the power of the elite crimson mage—which reached he soil of Amalia's grave first. Mayhara's long, dark waves danced around her lovely oval face, the wind causing the ends of her hair to play with her full lips.

The crimson particles were next joined by the copper glow of Shiro's power—the power of the elite copper mage. The glow mirrored the copper tips of his slightly disheveled black hair. Though Shiro stood with squared shoulders and a solid stance, there was a softness in his eyes—a sadness—that Karina couldn't miss.

The red and orange flow of magic now swirled with the golden glow of Salina's particles. The elite golden mage had her eyes narrowed as the wind tousled her golden-highlighted curls against the dark skin of her high cheek bones.

Loni—the elite emerald mage—pushed out her powers, the glowing green particles floating in to join the red, orange, and gold. Sweat glistened at her temples, dampening the black hair framing her face. Karina wasn't sure what demons Loni was struggling with, but she suspected Loni was doing her best to conquer them.

The bright blue glow of Jae's sapphire particles swept in and spiraled around the wave of the other magical molecules, joining the surge as the massive collection of magic entered the ground. Jae was the newest elite, having inherited the station when their friend Kamal was killed. But Jae had another connection to the prophecy that linked the two ancient deities responsible for the war that could end the world. Jae's sister, Naree, was also the reincarnation of the divine goddess Lakshmi. Of all the mages, Jae must have the most intense personal struggle with this war.

The last mage to infuse her powers into the strain was Yuki. She was the youngest elite mage, and as a diamond mage, also one of the rarest. Yuki looked so small, her auburn hair coming loose from her hair band, and wind made her black blouse and skirt thrash around her petite form.

Karina recited the lines of the incantation once more, raising her hands higher and opening her mind to receive the flow of magic.

It started slowly, a mild weakness in her legs. She forced herself to stand straight and hold her stance, fearing that she'd crumple to the ground if she gave in. Her body felt as if it were being hit with flashes of extreme hot and cold, and she found it difficult to breathe as light-headedness set in.

Tunnel vision caused her to focus on the bright light surfacing from her grandmother's grave. The glittering white light hovered over the grave for a moment and then seemed to be sucked into Karina's skin. Tiny pin pricks covered her body. She heard a ringing in her ears, and the wind picked up violently, the blast of it causing her eyes to water.

And somewhere in her head, she could swear she heard her grandmother's voice, but she couldn't make out the words.

The flames of the candles each of the mages carried

went out all at once, and Karina felt every muscle in her body tense.

The wind suddenly died, and Karina could feel a warm glow in her chest—a glow that seemed to slowly grow and expand until it filled every inch of her being.

Is this it? she wondered. Is the transfer complete?

A gasp from Loni snapped her out of her shock. Karina turned to see Loni gaping at a figure just out of her line of vision.

"Penny?" Salina said, shaking her head, her eyes wide.

Karina turned to see if it was, indeed, their long-lost amethyst mage, but the movement and the shift of balance overwhelmed her, and she felt herself falling to the ground.

In case you missed them…

Be sure to check out first four books in the

Empire of the Lotus series:

Available from all online retailers

CRIMSON MAGE

http://books2read.com/crimsonmage

COPPER MAGE

http://books2read.com/coppermage

GOLDEN MAGE

http://books2read.com/goldenmage

EMERALD MAGE

http://books2read.com/emeraldmage

ACKNOWLEDGEMENTS

It's hard to believe there are only two more books in this series. I feel as if my characters have endured a long, exiting journey that will soon be coming to a head. I have to say I've gone fond of them and look forward to wrapping up their destinies.

Of course, none of this would have been possible if I didn't have wonderful people in my corner supporting me. I'm eternally thankful to all my tribes and all they do to keep me going—especially during these trying times of a pandemic. The world is a crazy place, and it makes writing fiction like this seem not so far-fetched.

Wouldn't it be nice to be saved from all this chaos by some magical beings who want the world to be filled with peace?

Maybe one day.

ABOUT THE AUTHOR

Dorothy Dreyer is a Philippine-born American living in Germany with her husband, her two college kids, and two Siberian Huskies. She is an award-winning, *USA Today* Bestselling Author of young adult and new adult books that usually have some element of magic or the supernatural in them. Aside from reading, she enjoys movies, binge-watching series, chocolate, take-out, traveling, and having fun with friends and family.

You can find out more about Dorothy on her website: http://dorothydreyer.com

Like YA Fantasy?
Check out the award-winning CURSE OF THE
PHOENIX duology:

PHOENIX DESCENDING
http://books2read.com/phoenixdescending

Solo Medalist winner of the 2018 New Apple
Summer eBook awards in the category
Young Adult Fantasy

Who must she become in order to survive?

Since the outbreak of the phoenix fever in Drothidia, Tori
Kagari has already lost one family member to the fatal
disease. Now, with the fever threatening to wipe out her
entire family, she must go against everything she believes
in order to save them—even if that means making a deal
with the enemy.

When Tori agrees to join forces with the unscrupulous
Khadulians, she must take on a false identity in order to

infiltrate the queendom of Avarell and fulfill her part of the bargain, all while under the watchful eye of the unforgiving Queen's Guard. But time is running out, and every lie, theft, and abduction she is forced to carry out may not be enough to free her family or herself from death.

And …

PARAGON RISING
http://books2read.com/paragonrising

Book Two

in the

Curse of the Phoenix duology

On the brink of war, the fate of the nine realms lies in Tori Kagari's hands. After her arduous efforts to infiltrate the queendom of Avarell, Tori must now escape from it in an unforeseen alliance with a runaway princess and the soldier who saved Tori's life.

When the savage forces of Nostidour take hold of Avarell, Tori must seek out the rulers of the other realms and convince them to join the fight. But when the other realms discover that Tori has been lying about who she is, they are hesitant to trust her. Now Tori must find a way to prove herself, even if it means leading the battle herself and risking everything in the name of peace.

To keep them apart, the demons must convince Quinn that Aaron will betray her or, worse, confirm her fear that she's crazy. Aaron and Quinn's combined powers could banish the darkness for good, but only if she learns to trust her heart and he recovers the secret locked away in his fragile memory. That is, unless the demons kill them first.

ALL THE TALES WE TELL

by Annie Cosby

https://books2read.com/u/3nvO6P

She's filthy rich. He's not. It'll take patience, an old woman who thinks she's a selkie, and one salty-sweet summer on the beach to make them realize what's between them.

When Cora's mother whisks the family away for the summer, Cora must decide between forging her future in the glimmering world of second homes where her parents belong, or getting lost in the enchanting world of the locals and the mystery surrounding a lonely old woman who claims to be a selkie—and who probably needs Cora more than anyone else.

Through the fantastical tales and anguished memories of the batty Mrs. O'Leary, as well as the company of a particularly gorgeous local boy called Ronan, Cora finds an escape from the reality of planning her life after high school. But will it come at the cost of alienating Cora's mother, who struggles with her own tragic memories?

As the summer wanes, it becomes apparent that Mrs. O'Leary is desperate to leave Oyster Beach. And Ronan just may hold the answer to her tragic past— and Cora's future.

FANGS AND FINS

by Amy McNulty

https://books2read.com/b/boYLaL

A sleepy town hiding an ancient war. Two teenagers stuck in the middle. Will graduation be a permanent end?

Bookworm Ember Goodwin was looking for romance her senior year, not a new, popular-girl stepsister. And things get heated when a mesmerizing stranger in sunglasses vies for their attention. But when Ember wakes with a thirst for blood, she discovers her dreamy beau is hiding a supernatural-sized secret that could leave her sleeping in a coffin.

Queen bee Ivy Sheppard wishes her dad hadn't moved them in with his new wife just in time for her final year of high school. But when a budding romance with an aquatically gifted hunk leaves her with icy abilities, her unstable world turns upside down. Because an ancient feud is about to pit her against her nerdy stepsister in a fierce fight to the death.

Swept off her feet and growing in power, Ember will do anything for her undead boyfriend. But Ivy vows to put a stop to the paranormal mayhem before their newly blended family loses a daughter.

Will the two young women forge peace between warring magical worlds… or die for the ones they love?